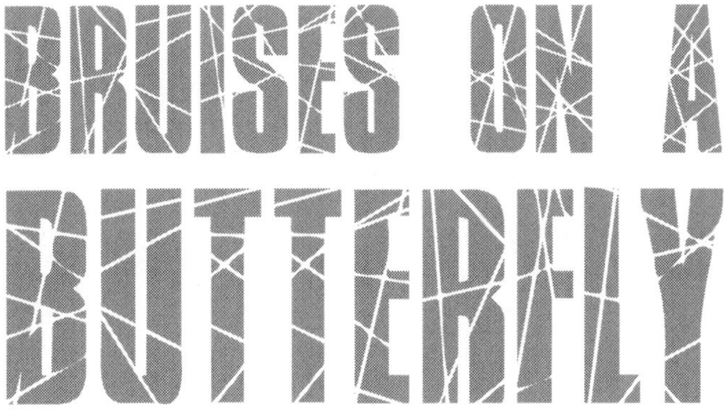
BRUISES ON A
BUTTERFLY

CHAD LUTZKE

CEMETERY DANCE PUBLICATIONS

Baltimore

2024

Cemetery Dance Publications
132B Industry Lane, Unit #7
Forest Hill, MD 21050
www.cemeterydance.com

Trade Paperback Edition

ISBN:
978-1-58767-954-4

Kids think stupid shit.
They do stupid shit, even when they mean well.
This is one of those times.

PROLOGUE

THE TWO YOUNG teens stood in the cemetery, a headstone at their feet. They'd visited the grave often that month, taking turns reading out loud from a book. This time, they read the final page and one set the book on the stone.

The other boy dug a small hole in the ground with a spoon, just deep enough to bury three sheets of paper folded several times over, like some hidden message that mustn't be found, then covered it with dirt and grass and said, "Your best one yet."

Last summer, they hadn't been teens yet, and none of them should have had to deal with what went down. They were supposed to be running through fields with pockets full of dirt, rolling down hills with dizzying heads, riding bikes on trails they'd made by hand, and most of all, sitting in their fort, reading comics and telling stories.

Not contemplating killing one of their own.

CHAPTER 1

TAYLOR SINGLETREE SCRUBBED at the dried oatmeal in the bowl he'd left under his bed. Soaking it in the sink wasn't an option. His dad would see it, and he'd know. He'd know damn well Taylor had done exactly what he'd been told not to.

"For every time you eat in your room, that's one meal skipped. Now you think about that!"

He does think about it. He thinks about it all the time, except when he forgets.

"And Lord knows, your scrawny ass can't afford to skip a meal."

He dug at the dried food with his fingernail, until he drove a piece under it. It felt like the splinter he'd gotten last month, when he and Kevin Clements had put up the very first wall in their fort. The plywood had slipped, and a tiny slice went under his nail, nearly down to the quick. The oatmeal sliver wasn't nearly as bad, but it reminded him of it.

He heard the alarm clock in his father's room go off.

In a panic, he grabbed a spoon from the drawer and scraped away at the bowl, as hot water poured from the faucet, weakening the food's grip.

"Taylor!" his dad called from somewhere in the house. Taylor swung around with the bowl in his hand, lost his hold, and splashed water everywhere. The bowl hit the refrigerator and shattered. "Put my coffee in the— What the fuck was that?"

"S...sorry, Dad!"

"What was it?"

There was no way out of it. The sound of something breaking is universally recognized by every parent on the planet, regardless of the distance between them and the crash. If they heard it, they knew exactly what it was.

Taylor took a deep breath and closed his eyes. "I broke a dish."

Then the footsteps came, purposely loud and meant to intimidate—a cannibalistic giant who's come to exact revenge.

Taylor ran to collect the pieces, showing he cared about the bowl, that he realized it cost money and money doesn't grow on trees. But it wouldn't matter.

The boy felt the neck of his shirt cinch tight. A backhand came first, knocking Taylor's glasses off. If they broke, that'd be his fault too.

"You clumsy piece of shit," the giant said through nicotine-stained teeth that squeaked while gritting. "Every fuckin' day it's something else with you. Breakin' shit, losin' shit."

"I'm sorry, Dad. It was an accident." Taylor covered his face, anticipating another blow.

"I don't wanna have to worry about this kind of bullshit while I'm at work. I should just lock your ass up while I'm gone."

"I'll clean it up, Dad. And I'll buy another one...from Goodwill."

"Yeah? With what money?"

"Jackie and I collected bottles last week." It was a half-truth. He and Jackie *had* collected bottles, enough to buy a two-liter of soda and a bag of pretzels, which they'd polished off that same afternoon. The money he had now was from a five-dollar bill he'd found in the parking lot of the convenience store. But he'd never tell his father that because no way in hell he'd believe it. He would accuse him of stealing. Something Taylor has never considered doing.

Jacob Singletree glared at his son on the kitchen floor, his child's one arm over his bowl-cut head, pencil legs tucked to his chest.

"Get up, pussy." Jacob kicked at Taylor's foot. "And make my coffee. You've got me runnin' late now." Jacob stormed back to his bedroom and slammed the door, while Taylor scrambled around the kitchen to make the perfect cup of coffee.

CHAPTER 2

KEVIN CLEMENTS PLUCKED a sausage patty from the plate before his mom had a chance to set it down.

"You'd think I starve you," his mother said.

The patties were just right. She even drizzled maple syrup over them—something Kevin had learned he loved by accident.

He wasn't as hungry as he was anxious to get out to Wagner's cornfield to meet Taylor and Jackie. After an hour-long meeting filled with distractions of every kind, they'd finally settled on a name for the fort. All that was left was the christening with a handmade sign, one he'd made with his father's drill, a length of rope, and a thick plank of wood they'd found on the side of the road.

Kevin's dad had helped with the sign, drilling the two holes, and even throwing on a coat of protective finish. Kevin did the rest—sanded the edges, looped the rope through, and painted the fort's title in black. Having the sign finished felt like things were finally official.

With the fort built, it was a great summer to be alive and young and full of piss and vinegar, as his grandfather often said. What was so special about a concoction of urine and something as godawful as vinegar had been a topic for discussion more than once between the boys, which ultimately led to the filling of an empty 2-liter—one half filled with vinegar, and the other with piss from all three of them. The dark yellow mixture sat on top of the fort, baking in the sun day after day as a reminder of the deal they'd made: the first to tell anyone about the fort—excluding parents, of course—the guilty party would have to drink the contents.

Taylor hadn't even bothered to tell his dad, but Kevin had already broken the rule when he spilled the secret to Father MacNaughton during confession, wherein he also mentioned peeking into Ms. Neil's bedroom window one night on his way home and seeing her naked. The guilt haunted him for weeks, and the memory of her pink nipples reared its shameful head every moment he was alone in bed.

Kevin downed the rest of his food and ran for his safe haven, the garage. More times than he could count, while in bed, he would set his pillow on the windowsill and rest his head there, gazing at the light that spilled from the garage's gaping mouth like a small piece of sunshine, as his dad worked inside on all number of things. The sounds that poured from within held more serenity than crickets—a mechanical lullaby that would send the boy into a peaceful slumber every time.

Occasionally, he would wander out and help his dad on whatever project the man toiled over. Doing a grown-man's work in his pajamas when he should be in bed made him feel special and older.

Kevin grabbed the fort's sign, straddled his BMX bike, and coasted down the driveway, his feet dangling. He stopped when he saw Kristy Spencer across the street watering a dead patch of grass in the center of her lawn. Kristy was the one he vowed to marry, or at least kiss. It started as a joke between him, Taylor, and Jackie. But then one day, the blonde-haired girl smiled at him, directly *at* him. Just him. That smile turned a joke into legitimate desire, and from that moment on, whenever she was around, his mouth went dry and his stomach filled with thumbtacks.

He raised a hand to say a silent hello, but it went unnoticed, so he ran his fingers through the sandy mess on his head, then coasted toward her.

"Hi, Kristy."

Her head swiveled with surprise, then she smiled. "Oh...hey, Kevin."

"The lawn looks good."

Kristy chuckled. "Thanks."

"Doing chores, huh?"

"Yep."

Kevin already regretted every word. The uncomfortable silence between them was an elephant the size of Texas.

"What's that?" Kristy pointed toward the wooden sign.

Kevin hid the words with his leg. "Just a piece of wood."

"You building something with your dad?"

"Yeah. We're making a doghouse." Kevin hated lying, and what he really wanted to do was ask if she wanted to see the fort, maybe even come and watch the christening. But that meant drinking the vinegar-piss, and he wasn't sure a girl was worth that. Even if it *was* Kristy Spencer.

Kristy squinted her eyes, as though doing so would pull the truth from him. "Well... have fun," she said, then went back to watering the lawn, dismissing him.

Kevin's face burned red hot, as though the sun had moved closer than it had any right to. "You too."

He pedaled away and spent the whole ride to Wagner's field reciting everything he *should* have said, damning the perfect words that always came too late.

CHAPTER 3

JACKIE HARTFORD RAN back inside with a Tiger lily in his hand. He stood at the counter catching his breath, then wiped the sweaty curls from his forehead and cursed the hindering chub around his waist. He stuck the flower in a small vase filled with water and placed the vase on a TV tray next to a bowl of Rice Krispies and cold cinnamon toast, fixed the placement of the toast so it was symmetrical, then carried the food down the hall to a bedroom door left ajar.

He pushed the door with his foot, opening it to a dimly lit room, glowing amber from the morning sun. It was Jackie's favorite room in the house, not just because of the calming hue, but because of the good times had within—tickling sessions, late night monster movies while covered in popcorn, and important talks, like why his dad *really* left and how to deal with bullies on an intellectual level. He valued those talks. And during the movies, he would sometimes pretend to fall asleep just so he wouldn't have to leave for his own bed. His mother would wrap an arm around him and cover the back of his head with a thousand kisses. Despite the good times and shared laughter, he knew she felt far more alone than she let on.

On that beautiful sunny morning, Rhonda Hartford slept on her side, their Chihuahua, Furley, curled behind her knees. The dog was a stray that Jackie had brought home three years before. It took no convincing at all for his mother to agree to keep him after failing to find its owner.

Jackie set the tray on the bed and drew back the curtains. Venetian blinds cut the morning light into thin strips across the room.

Furley stretched, yawned. Rhonda stirred awake, opened one eye, squinted the other. "You want me to melt?"

"You won't melt."

"I'm the Incredible Melting Woman."

Jackie laughed heartily and grabbed the tray. "Sit up."

"Wow...look at this. I feel like a queen." Slowly, Rhonda sat up, propping the pillows behind her, while Furley found another place on the bed to curl up.

"The Incredible Melting Queen." Jackie placed the tray carefully on her lap. "Happy birthday, Mom."

Her face filled with wrinkles as her smile broadened. "Thank you, honey." She put her nose to the flower, inhaled deeply. "Doesn't smell like tigers."

Jackie rolled his eyes at the joke that's been told too many times, and a bit too childish for a 12-year-old boy who'd recently found hair under his arms.

A figure outside the window caught Rhonda's eye. It was their neighbor, Mrs. Degraves, walking briskly toward their front door, a furrowed brow and accompanying frown that seemed to melt her own face.

"Shit, Jackie. Where'd you get the flower?"

"She has hundreds of 'em."

"You can't just—"

A knock on the door.

Jackie held his breath and stood statue-still, locking eyes with his mother. The two gazed at one another but neither moved. Finally, his mother's stone mask broke as a smirk crept its way through her tightened lips.

"I suppose she can spare just one." Her smile went full force, and Jackie let out a sigh of relief.

Another knock at the door and his mother put a finger to her lips, shushing him. One more angry knock, and the Venetian-split figure of Mrs. Degraves shambled back home.

"It was a beautiful gesture, Jackie, but no more. Okay?"

"Until Mother's Day," he joked.

"So...what are your plans today?" Rhonda smelled the flower once more, then grabbed a piece of toast and took a bite.

"No plans."

Rhonda raised an eyebrow and swallowed a piece of toast that could have used a little more butter. "I bet I know what you *think* you're doing."

"What? What am I doing?"

"Dedicating your day to me as a gift."

"Well...it's the only gift I've got."

"Jackie, you've started my day with a smile, and that's good enough for me."

"Good. Let's keep the smile going." He went to the blinds and raised them. The strips of light disappeared along with the amber glow, and the whole room filled with Southwest Michigan sunshine.

"What would keep me smiling is knowing you're with Kevin and Taylor, building your fort, while I bury my face in a book."

Jackie looked at his mother, trying to read her, making sure it's what she really wanted. She hid her pain so well sometimes.

"You're just gonna read all day?" He pulled his shirt down, a nervous habit he had, making sure his belly was always covered. His mother took notice.

"I love that belly, kiddo. And you should too."

Embarrassed, Jackie looked down, pinched the extra 10 pounds or so he could stand to lose. "It makes me slow, I think. I don't run as fast as Kevin or Taylor. Or even June Ackels."

"That's because her legs are too long. She's like an ostrich." Rhonda took another bite of toast and playfully shooed him away. "Go have fun."

He studied her again, making sure. Taylor had once told him some people were inter-verts and they liked to be alone, and that they got tired when around other people. It made no sense to Jackie, but Taylor was the reader, the smartest of the three. He always had a name for everything they didn't. So, he believed him. Even if it sounded like bullshit.

"You sure?"

"Absolutely. Now go get dressed so I can eat this wonderful breakfast you made."

Jackie began backing out of the room with comical slowness.

"Get!"

Ten minutes later, Jackie was on his bike, heading toward Wagner's field.

CHAPTER 4

TAYLOR LOOKED IN the bathroom mirror. There was a red dot on the side of his nose where his glasses had broken the skin, a growing bruise surrounding it. His dad had left for work without another word, perfect cup of coffee in hand.

On Taylor's bedroom wall was a checklist of chores he'd write daily—a reminder never to forget a single one of them. Or else. He stuck his middle finger up at the list and walked away, then cowered back to it and made note of the first chore:

Clean your room.

His room was rarely dirty. Certainly, dishes were never left in there. Almost never. And he didn't own enough to make a mess. He had a dresser for his clothes, his mother's favorite ashtray (a ceramic dragon), a nightstand with a lamp, and one bookshelf. His pride and joy.

There were only a dozen books on the shelf he hadn't read yet, one of those being *The Thief of Always* by his favorite author, Clive Barker. He hadn't read it yet because he sensed it may be the author's best one yet. The gorgeous artwork by Clive himself pulled at him daily, but the thought of never having it to look forward to, of having already discovered the strange world inside, kept the pages closed. It would have to be a very special occasion, like an aged wine that's kept in the cellar for a celebration too big to ignore.

The books were organized first by genre, then alphabetically. Adventure, fantasy, horror, mystery, and science fiction. He loved them all, and not even bamboo shoots under his nails could get him to confess a favorite. Each had their own world to escape to. Some made him cry, some made him leap with joy, some scared him, some brought a tingle of excitement, and he liked to pretend each of those worlds existed somewhere outside Springview, Michigan.

He stood in his room, looked around, then ran and got a wet washcloth from the kitchen and wiped down the nightstand, dresser, and shelves. After putting the washcloth back, he checked "clean your room" off the list.

He was supposed to meet Kevin and Jackie at the fort in less than twenty minutes, but the draw of creativity pulled, and when it did, he would always succumb. If he didn't, he would never become a writer—the most important thing in the world—with a shelf full of his own books.

Taylor lifted his mattress and retrieved the notepad underneath, pulled the pen from within the metal spiral, and threw himself on the bed. As he flipped through the scribbled pages, his eyes went blurry, flooding with tears. His life was so much different than his friend's. Staying the night with them was always bittersweet. The first night he ever stayed at Kevin's, he and Kevin got in a fight. It was Taylor's fault. He found himself jealous and couldn't figure out why. He cried himself to sleep that night and apologized the next day, telling Kevin, "I guess I want what you have. This bedroom, the toys, that kickass meal your mom cooked last night. A dad who doesn't… just… a different dad, I guess."

"What's mine is yours, bro," was all Kevin said, and it seemed to be enough.

Now, with the notebook open and pen in hand, he brushed the tears away, took a deep breath, and began to write:

The malnourished boy looked out the barred window and stared into the sun. He did this sometimes. "Either save me or burn me," he told it. "Burn the whole castle, and everything in it."

He wanted so badly to rip the bars from the thick, brick wall, but his muscles were weak from years of imprisonment.

The heavy footsteps outside his cell startled him, and he scurried to the door. He peeked through the small hole in it and saw the beast's claws as they slipped a key into a padlock the size of a catcher's mitt.

"It's time to eat," the beast growled.

The chain rattled, then fell to the dungeon floor. The boy backed away and took his place on the bed. A bed he'd spent more nights on than he could count, tossing and turning, and planning his escape.

The door opened, and the smell of steamy gruel filled the small room.

The beast set the bowl on the dirty floor. "Enough with the sun." he said. "Eat and go to sleep. I'll be back for the bowl. And don't break it!"

The door slammed, the chains rattled, and the lock shut. But the boy had a plan, and it all started with the bowl of gruel.

CHAPTER 5

KEVIN SAT ON the flat, wooden roof of the fort with his hand over his eyes to block the sun. He searched for any movement along the corn rows, be it his friends or an approaching enemy.

His eyes trailed to the far tree line where they would park their bikes under the evergreens. Riding a bike between the rows—handlebars ripping at the stalks of corn—would leave a visible trail, and it was important to keep the path concealed as much as possible.

The pine forest was like another world entirely—a dark green rectangle that kept itself hidden from the sun. The perfect place for shade—and pine needles for kindling—the few times they'd made a fire for cooking hotdogs, chicken, or fish they'd caught at Goguac Lake, something they'd never do again. After having spent half the day in the hot sun, Jackie threw up after only one bite of bluegill. Kevin insisted Jackie's piece of fish wasn't fully cooked, where Taylor blamed the heat, stating Jackie may have suffered from heatstroke. Either way, fish was now off the menu.

The 2-liter bottle of vinegar-piss sat next to Kevin, the sides of which no longer had any give, as though carbonated and factory sealed. If an enemy ever did approach their secret sanctuary, it'd make for one hell of a makeshift bomb, exploding when it met the ground, and spreading the malodorous contents like vomit-inducing shrapnel.

Mornings like this were the best. A stomach full of food, a robin's egg blue sky, and a lifetime of hours still left in the day. A lot would get accomplished, most importantly the christening.

As Kevin squinted, he could make out movement of the cornstalks in the distance. "Caccaw!" He did his best crow impression, which was laughable between the three of them. The shifting corn stopped, and the impression was echoed, much better than his own. It was Jackie. Kevin could tell by how realistic the sound, as though he were born half bird. Or the kid practiced in his room just for the occasion, which was easy to believe considering the call was Jackie's idea.

Kevin climbed down the side of the fort using the four-step ladder they'd made out of wood from Wagner's barn. It was an old barn, and they'd gotten permission. They'd even been granted permission to build their fort in the middle of his field, and when harvest time came, he made sure to work around the area, like the fort was some immovable rock stuck in the earth, or an old oak tree that held too many memories to ever consider chopping down on account of a few dozen extra ears of corn per year.

Jackie walked out of the corn rows and into the half-dirt/half-grass area surrounding the fort. "I know…I know. I'm runnin' late."

"You're not the only one," Kevin said."

"Where's Taylor?"

"Dunno."

The two boys looked at the ground in silence while a multitude of scenarios ran through their heads, none of them good, all of them involving Taylor's dad.

"I fucking hate him." Jackie said.

"Yep."

They'd witnessed enough of Jacob Singletree's bullshit to have concern for their friend. And with him running late, those scenarios were hard to keep at bay, like two worried fathers wondering why their child is an hour past curfew.

Then, like some beautiful songbird revealing all was okay, the unmistakable caw of a mediocre imitation crow was heard in the distance. Both boys, visibly relieved, ran down the designated row of corn meant for travel—the thirteenth row from the white pine with the broken limb.

Jackie gave his best caw back, and the boys met in the middle of the field. The smiles Jackie and Kevin wore slowly faded when they saw Taylor's nose, but did their best not to bring attention to it. Taylor wouldn't say a word, and neither would they. That's the way it always was, except for the time Mr. Singletree broke Taylor's nose, which left a small, permanent bump that, thankfully, was only noticeable in just the right light. That day, Taylor had told them everything, about how the dog pissed in the house and Taylor had been blamed for not letting him out enough, when in fact he let the dog out every hour. But it wasn't a fist that broke Taylor's nose. It was his father's work boot, a kick meant for the ribs after pushing Taylor down into the dog's mess. The next day, his father apologized by ordering a pizza and letting him eat it in his room, alone. A week later, Taylor found the dog dead in his backyard behind the shed.

That was the last time Taylor ever mentioned abuse, though his friends knew there was more, that it hadn't stopped, and the occasional mark or somber mood was evidence of such.

"You ready?" Kevin pulled attention away from the obvious.

"Did you bring the sign?" Taylor asked.

"In the fort."

Taylor's eyes lit up like nothing else mattered. Nothing but the christening.

Single file, the three boys hurried to the fort. It was like Christmas. They'd gone through several names, making a long list of dozens. After boiling it down to their favorite three, the names were tossed into a baseball cap, and one was randomly drawn for their fortress in the corn.

"You went with the same title, right?" Jackie asked.

"Of course." Kevin flicked the eye hook attached to the fort and opened the door.

Taylor entered first, then Jackie and Kevin. The fort itself was a perfect 8 x 8-foot square with a 6-foot ceiling and a hinged piece of wood in the back to create a window that opened like a small door and kept shut by an eye hook.

The bulk of it was built from two-by-fours and plywood, supplied mostly by Kevin's dad, Mr. Wagner, and an old lemonade stand Jackie had stopped using when he was ten. The door itself was an oil-stained piece of wood which Hazel Automotive once used in their garage, giving the fort a "rugged, manly" scent, according to Kevin. The floor remained as is—dirt, flattened by a million footsteps.

A brown vinyl beanbag chair sat in one corner, a milk crate in another, and on the back wall under the window, a lidded bench made from scrap wood and cushions from an old pontoon boat Jackie had found at a garage sale. There, in the middle of the bench, sat the new sign with its official title in all its glory.

The Pantheon II.

"You sure about the Roman numerals?" Jackie asked.

"It's named after a Roman temple. Of course, I'm sure. Plus, it looks cool like that," Taylor said.

"I know, but what if someone thinks it says eleven?"

"Who else is going to see it?" Kevin looked at Jackie with a raised eyebrow.

"Good point."

"Let the christening begin." Kevin grabbed the sign and went outside. Taylor followed, while Jackie lifted the bench seat and grabbed a single can of Budweiser stashed within.

The nail had already been placed last week, just to the right of the door. Kevin lifted the sign and tossed the rope over the nail, and if there were ever a choir of angels with a reason to sing, now would be the time.

"By the power vested in us," Taylor said. "We dub thee—"

And the words *Pantheon Two* were said in unison among the trio.

Jackie shook the can of beer, pointed it toward the sign, and pulled the tab. Foamy brew sprayed the sign, the fort, and the boys, then Jackie took a sip and passed the can to Kevin.

Jackie's face went sour, and he spit the beer out. "People drink that shit?"

Kevin took a sip and followed suite. He started to hand the beer to Taylor, then said, "You don't have to, dude."

"I can handle it." Taylor grabbed the can.

"I mean if you think you might get in trouble. Maybe your old man will smell it on you."

Taylor chuckled. "When you practically wear it as cologne, it's hard to smell on anyone else." He took a sip and swallowed. The other two looked at him incredulously. "What? I've had some before."

"You've drank beer before?" Kevin asked, stunned.

"Yeah. I got curious, wondered what the fuss was about and why my dad couldn't live without it."

"So, you like it?" Jackie asked.

"No. It tastes like shit."

All three of them laughed, wiping the beer from their lips.

"To The Pantheon Two." Taylor raised the beer in toast, took a sip and passed it. The other two stomached another round, then burped as loud as they could.

"Aren't we supposed to pour some on the ground?" Jackie asked.

"No. That's something else," Taylor said. "It's like a message to the dead, I think."

"Huh."

"We did it, boys." Kevin said. "We actually did it."

They planted their eyes on the sign and the fort behind it. And if their smiles were any wider, their lips would split.

JACKIE was smoothing out the piece of duct tape used to cover a hole in the beanbag as he sat in it, the sides not as bulgy as they once were. "It's a classic scam. You say you're staying the night at my house. I say I'm staying at yours, and Taylor says yours too. It's a true christening. A consummation."

Kevin burst out in a fit of laughter, holding his gut, and rocking back on the milk crate.

"What?"

Kevin caught his breath. "I don't think you know what consummation means."

"It means crashing here will be the final touch on the christening." Jackie said.

"It means sex dude. It means banging your wife on your wedding night."

"It doesn't always mean that," Taylor said. "It's anything that finalizes something." And that's all it took to shut Kevin down. If anyone knew what a word meant, it was Taylor. "I'll do it. I'll stay here tonight."

Jackie's eyes grew like two big moons, then he turned their glow on Kevin. "Well?"

"Tay…if you get caught—"

"I'm not gonna get caught." His tone was full of confidence.

"Okay, I'll do it too." Kevin said. "We'll meet here at 8:00. I'll bring Doritos and bread. Jackie, you bring the Mountain Dew. Tay, you bring the best story you've got. Something really scary."

"Hell yes! We're really doing this, aren't we?" Jackie threw his fist in the air and jumped out of the beanbag, excited for the night ahead.

Taylor just smiled—a tight-lipped thing that lacked the assurance he'd shown only a moment before. His dad rarely cared where he went, and any time he stayed the night somewhere, his dad never asked for details. There was never a request to meet the parents or for the phone number, but his dad seemed to have a sixth sense when being lied to, like the time Taylor left an empty bottle of beer in the driveway and his dad ran over it, flattening his tire. The man studied that bottle like it was the rarest of fossils, then pointed out the black residue around the top of it. "You lying piece of shit. You used this to shoot off rockets. That's why it was sitting out here." Along with a two-week grounding, Taylor was smacked in the back of the head so hard he bit through his tongue. Any other parent would have taken their child for stitches. Jacob Singletree told him suck it up, spit the blood, and take a sip of whiskey if need be.

If he was going to lie about tonight, it better be a night to remember.

CHAPTER 6

TAYLOR HAD A five-minute conversation with his father in the small window of time between the end of his dad's shift at work and heading to the bar. It consisted of bitching about the smell of Taylor's shoes, the lack of air circulating through the house—"Leave the fuckin' windows open!"— and Taylor saying he's going to stay the night at Kevin's.

Getting permission to stay the night was never an issue. He was never told he couldn't. Taylor figured it was because any chance his dad had of getting rid of him, he'd take it. One time, Taylor stayed two nights in a row at Jackie's but had asked to stay only one. His dad never noticed. But the lie and that damn sixth sense. That could seal his fate.

But as his dad walked out the door on his way to the bar, letting the screen slam against its rotting frame, something snapped in Taylor. He knew the word for what that snap was. He'd used it before, but never with such a profoundness behind it.

Epiphany.

It was the perfect word for his revelation: that life didn't have to be like this. The home that was quickly falling apart, with its bacheloresque aesthetic and its scum-of-the-earth owner who used him as a punching bag. He would be a teenager soon. A young man. Before he moved from his spot where he stood frozen in the kitchen, staring at the screen door, still hearing its echo, he thought of the freedom ahead. And it scared the shit out of him.

He ran to his room and packed his notepad filled with the stories he'd written, and his copy of *The Thief of Always*, then went to his father's bedroom—a pigsty that made any lazy teen look good. The curtains, having been pulled down more than once under drunken feet, were nailed above the windows. An ashtray sat on the dresser and another on his nightstand, both piled high with Marlboros smoked down to melted filters. Clothes were strewn about across the bed, in the bottom of the closet, and over the door. An open pizza box stuck out from under the bed with two dried pieces inside, curled at the ends.

Within the open nightstand was an impressive stack of smut: Penthouse, Hustler, Oui, and Barely Legal. Taylor grabbed the one on the very bottom. Penthouse. He sat on his dad's bed, flipped through it. The photos were strangely fuzzy, like the women were standing behind a thin sheet of fog, but he supposed it somehow made them prettier. He'd seen the same effect on Star Trek reruns or movies from the 70s, normally in the scenes where they showed women.

The pictures did nothing for him. He'd sat among Jackie and Kevin before when they'd talk about scenes from rated R movies (or even some PG ones) where they showed tits and ass and the two would argue on whose was the best, but Taylor found no interest in such discussions. He supposed maybe he was broken, or maybe just so used to seeing it around the house.

He took one last look at a pair of foggy breasts, shrugged his weighted shoulders, and closed the magazine, then tossed it in his backpack and headed to the living room, where he sat on the couch with his notebook. He pulled the pen from the spine, and in his best handwriting wrote:

Dear Jacob,

Fuck you!

Then he taped the note to the refrigerator door using four wide strips of duct tape, making sure the statement would stay. The note was a trigger being pulled. Once his father saw it, there was no turning back. And that's exactly why he did it, so he could never come home again only to find himself in a position he'd been in too many times before, crying in his room, wishing he could dive into one of the many worlds he read about in his books, far away from Jacob Singletree.

CHAPTER 7

THE BOY ATE *nearly the whole bowl of gruel. It tasted bad. Worse than beer. Worse than dandelion stems.*

When he was sure the beast wasn't near, he pulled a fingerful of the horrible stuff from the bowl and walked to the barred window. He could hear the birds sing, and the leaves rustling in the breeze. He looked to the sky. Clouds were approaching, like some giant bruise in the distance.

"Either save me or burn me," he pleaded with the sun, then scraped his finger on the outside of one of the bars, coating it with gruel.

Now he would wait, while cursing the growing bruise, praying it would somehow spread to nothing, giving the sun this moment to do what was needed.

CHAPTER 8

BY DINNERTIME, KEVIN had his stuff packed: Two bags of Doritos and a full loaf of bread he pulled from the chest freezer in the basement. He wanted to bring his pillow and blanket, but it might raise suspicion. He never took them when staying at Jackie's. Instead, he planned to use a pontoon cushion and bring a long-sleeve shirt just in case it got cold, which it wouldn't. It was still 80 degrees by the time he finished his mac and cheese.

After filling the dishwasher, Kevin went out to the garage, where his dad was varnishing a closet door and applying new hardware. It was from Kevin's closet and used to hold stickers. Mostly cartoon characters, a few of them random animals he'd gotten out of a magazine. Kevin had told his father only a month before: "I'll be a teenager soon, Dad. I'm getting too old for this kinda stuff. Can you get the stickers off?" His father chuckled. "I'm serious. What if I have a girl over one day. I can't be having Scooby Doo on here."

"Don't be so quick to grow up," his dad had said. "There may come a day when you'll wish you could relive these days, slow 'em down so they'd last twice as long."

Kevin doubted that.

"So, how'd your friends like the sign?" Joe Clements said as he ran a brush over the door that lay across two sawhorses, 70s light rock whispered from the radio on the work bench. The radio was dotted with tiny specks of paint like little yellow stars from when he painted the kitchen nearly ten years ago.

"They loved it. Looks great hanging up."

"You did a fine job with it, buddy."

"Thanks."

"Heading to Jackie's?"

Kevin hated lying even more when it was to his dad. His dad treated him with respect, like an adult. Never condescending, always trusting. What bothered Kevin most was there was so much about him his dad didn't know, like the half-pack of cigarettes he smoked (but no inhaling) with Taylor and Jackie, and that one cigar with Kevin Shea under the bleachers last spring break. Or the time he watched a rated R movie over at Jackie's house and paused it during the part where the girl took a shower, and of course about watching Ms. Neil undress—But he'd told Father MacNaughton about that one, so the guilt fizzled—And then today he drank real beer.

With his eyes falling on everything but his father, Kevin said, "Yep."

"I remember when I was a kid and had sleepovers. We wouldn't sleep a wink."

"Yeah?"

"Felt like crap the next day, but it was worth it. Lots of laughs, lots of memories." Joe kept his eyes on the door, making careful strokes down the wood.

"Do you and mom do that sometimes? Stay up all night?"

Joe laughed. "It's a lot tougher to pull off when you're older."

Movement across the street caught Kevin's attention. Kristy Spencer. She had a book in her hand, getting comfortable on the porch swing. He watched her a moment, not out of curiosity—he knew she read a lot, maybe even as much as Taylor—but because she stirred something in him he didn't quite understand, and the funny part was very little of it had to do with how beautiful she was. Something about her personality was maybe the most attractive bit. She actually paid attention to him, listened to him, looked in his eyes when he talked.

The distinction between outward and inward beauty and the dissection of it made Kevin think of a movie he'd seen once where one of the actresses was drop-dead gorgeous, like Farrah Fawcett gorgeous, Heather Thomas and Miss October gorgeous. But once you got to know the character and what a heartless bitch she was, the beauty faded like it was never there. Kristy wasn't like that. She had both inside *and* outside beauty.

"You're sweet on her, huh?" Joe said.

Kevin turned from Kristy like he'd been caught looking at a centerfold tacked to the wall.

"She's a nice girl. You've got good taste, just like your old man."

Kevin hated it when his dad said "old man." Old men shamble around in slippers and shit their pants and yell at kids for just having fun. Old men were close to dying. He didn't want to be fatherless, like Jackie. He wanted to make more signs and learn about tools and hear bad jokes and get embarrassed about girls. And if his dad *did* die, he'd feel the guilt of a thousand hells because he never told his father about the cigarettes and the pausing of nude scenes on the VCR, and the beer.

"She's alright," was all he said.

"Yeah, okay," his dad snickered.

Kevin watched his dad brush the varnish on. He liked the smell. It made him feel the same way the light pouring from the garage in the middle of the night did. "The door looks great, Dad. Thanks for doing that."

"Can't have Kristy seeing those stickers on there, can we?"

"Dad!" It was a near whisper, full of panic, like Kristy Spencer might hear them, put two and two together and never speak with him again. Or worse, laugh at the idea she would ever like him back, crushing Kevin's heart to an irreparable pulp.

"I'm just messin' with you." Joe smiled, and his face seemed to crack, reminding Kevin of old people. Reminding him of old people dying.

"Well… I better get going. The guys are waiting."

"Okay, buddy. Have fun. If you happen to stay up all night, take a nap tomorrow. Trust me. You'll feel a lot better."

Kevin forced a laugh. "I will. Thanks."

He slung the backpack over his shoulder and hopped on his bike, then coasted down the drive and caught a quick glimpse of Kristy as she read her book.

Before he'd passed her driveway, she yelled, "Hi, Kevin!"

Astonished, he turned and waved, his grin a ridiculous thing that belonged on the cover of Mad Magazine. He was pretty sure that was the first time Kristy was the one to initiate a greeting. For the next ten minutes, on his way to Wagner's field, that's all he could think about.

CHAPTER 9

RHONDA HARTFORD PULLED into the driveway with a car full of groceries. Jackie had stayed to do some chores, none of which he was asked to do, but it *was* his mother's birthday and he'd asked her to grab a couple 2 liters of Mountain Dew while she was out. So, he'd dusted the bookshelf, the coffee table, the end tables, and the TV, then vacuumed the living room and cleaned his bedroom. Well, mostly cleaned it. The closet remained cluttered, and instead of hanging his dress shirts, he had the habit of tossing them over the hanger bar. He also suspected more than a few pairs of underwear and socks lived under the bed along with gum, chip, and candy wrappers. Mostly clean.

He helped his mom carry in the groceries and take care of them. He spotted the frozen burritos and fish sticks and smiled. His mom didn't like buying them. She often complained about him not eating enough whole foods—whatever that meant—yet she always showed mercy with at least a few of his favorites. It helped make up for the bland cereal and wheat bread she insisted on buying.

Jackie reveled in the praise he received for cleaning the house and downed a few burritos covered in sour cream and salsa, then packed a gym bag filled with the 2 liters, a pair of shorts, and a battery-operated lantern using fresh batteries taken from his tape player. He nearly opted for the tape player instead, with the hopes of adding to the small stack of tapes he'd recorded where he and his friends put on audio skits, as well as a few of Taylor's ghost stories. But having a light source in the middle of a cornfield on a dark summer night made more sense.

Jackie grabbed the goods and headed toward the door. "Going to Kevin's!"

"Hold on. Didn't they get their number changed recently?"

The Clements *had* gotten their number changed. Their line had become a Grand Central Station for telemarketers, and one elderly man who insisted his wife lived at that number. The man would call during all hours of the night, asking for Abigail. It was bothersome for Kevin's parents, but for Kevin it was downright eerie, and his imagination went wild with theories of the house being haunted by the ghost of a senile man's wife. Every time the phone rang past midnight, Kevin's mind would wander, and every little sound became a ghost named Abigail, waiting for her husband to contact her.

"Yeah," Jackie said.

"Will you leave it on the fridge please?"

Shit.

Jackie set his bag down and went to the kitchen, opened the junk drawer, and pulled out a pad of sticky notes. Giving her the number felt like the beginning of the end. She would call to wish him goodnight or ask how much fun he's having, only to find he never even went to Kevin's. The parents would have a pow wow over where their kids might be. The police would get involved. And then Taylor's dad would be alerted, and he'd beat Taylor so bad he wouldn't show for school next fall because he'd have to learn to walk again.

While the risk of getting caught was great, he couldn't back out now. So, when writing Kevin's number on the paper, he sloppily wrote the fours and the nines as though they could be interchangeable. Should she try calling, she would chalk the ineligible writing up as an honest mistake and merely reprimand him on his penmanship. It was foolproof.

Satisfied with the crafty plan, Jackie stuck the note on the fridge, grabbed his bag, said goodbye, and actually whistled a tune on the way to his bike.

CHAPTER 10

AS THE SUN *hid behind a cover of clouds, the gruel sat drying on the bars that crossed the window of the dungeon cell. The boy touched the gruel. It was hard, like cement. Perfect. Now he just needed the rain to stay away in order for the next part of his plan to happen.*

As thunder roared in the distance, its booming sound matched the heavy footsteps of the beast as it walked toward the door. The boy plopped down on the mattress made from burlap and hay and slid the empty bowl toward the door. It was licked clean. It had to be. If it was not, he would be subject to torture of the worst kind. He survived it once but didn't think he could again.

The lock rattled and the key turned, then the thunder broke through, and the rain fell.

CHAPTER 11

WHEN KEVIN AND Jackie showed up at the fort, Taylor was already there, notebook in lap and writing. He'd spread blankets on the floor, each with their own pillow or cushion.

"Whoa," Kevin said. "Your dad let you bring these blankets?"

"They were my mom's. Been packed in the garage. He never goes out there."

The two boys dropped their goods and divvied them out, showing off the bread and Doritos and Mountain Dew. Taylor arranged them neatly in the corner.

Jackie looked up. "Dude! Where'd you get that?"

Thumbtacked to the back of the fort's door was the centerfold ripped from the issue of Penthouse Taylor had brought—a glowing blonde goddess with her legs spread, her labia barely hidden by a brown tuft of hair.

Kevin looked up, and a stone settled in his throat. He couldn't tear his gaze away. This was no grainy pausing of a VHS tape, with its obnoxious track lines in inconvenient places. This was clear and in your face, and so much more than breasts. So much more. "How?" Was the only word he could muster.

"Jacob has a whole stack of them," Taylor said.

"Jacob?" Jackie looked away from the poster long enough to cast a confused brow at his friend. "You mean your dad?"

"I don't call him that anymore."

"It looks like it's shiny down there." Kevin's eyes were still stuck. "Is it supposed to be shiny?"

Taylor laughed. "You've never seen a naked woman before?"

"Not down there."

"Here." Taylor lifted the bench and reached inside. He pulled the Penthouse from within. "Have fun."

"Holy shit!" Jackie said, grabbing the magazine.

Kevin seemed almost scared of it, as though it had teeth that meant to bite.

Jackie frantically flipped through the pages, never stopping long enough to take in a single image. It was a blur of flesh, all tan and shiny pink. When he reached the last page, he started over again, this time taking in each page, while Kevin peeked from above him, trying to act with a fraction of the interest he actually had.

Taylor watched in fascination at their reaction to something he saw every day of his life. On any given day, smut could be found on the back of the toilet, the porch, on the end-table near his dad's recliner, and even once on the front lawn after his dad passed out one Fourth of July—a half-eaten piece of pizza on his belly, and a copy of Barely Legal in the grass next to him.

Taylor shook his head, grabbed his notebook, and began to write.

CHAPTER 12

***THE BEAST OPENED** the door, and the room filled with the usual funk. The boy plugged his nose and breathed through his mouth, while meaty, clawed fingers pulled the empty bowl into the hall.*

He felt the sprinkle of rain on his back and whimpered at the realization that his plan had failed. The rain had softened the crusted gruel and was washing it away. It would take at least another day, maybe more, before the first part of his plan could work again.

"Quit yer crying, pussy," the beast roared. "Or I'll break your fingers, and you'll eat with your tongue like a dog."

The boy took a deep breath and held it. He'd had bones broken before at the hand of the beast and would not give him the satisfaction again. Instead of crying, he turned his hurt to rage and let it burn inside, while the door slammed, the chains rattled, and the key turned the lock once again.

CHAPTER 13

THE BOYS SPENT the rest of daylight gathering dead wood and kindling on the edge of the tree line. This wasn't their first fire, but it was their first at night, where it might be easily seen from afar. They'd gotten Mr. Wagner's blessing for daytime fires last year, after he stumbled upon them cooking skewered chicken wings. Taylor nearly cried, worrying his dad would find out. But Mr. Wagner had known all about his asshole father and this was the main reason he let the kids have their fort in the middle of his field, worked around it, and contributed what he could.

But this fire was at night, where the flames would cast long shadows that blackened the creepy spaces beyond the fire's light, where an ambush would be easy, be it beast or man. Jacob Singletree's hand could suddenly reach out and grasp one of their shoulders. Or it could be one of the beasts in Taylor's stories, like the woman with no mouth, who moaned behind a thin stretch of flesh, looking for those who wronged her.

The fire was lit, the shadows cast, and the three of them sat around it, sticks in hand, lighting the tips, then blowing them out. Crickets sang from the pines, and the occasional breeze rustled the cornstalk leaves. Every time it did, the boys froze, waiting for the ambush. Waiting for drunken, dirty hands and mumbling no-mouths.

"You still want to hear a story I wrote?" Taylor asked, knowing they didn't dare.

"Or we could talk about the crush Kevin has on Kristy Spencer."

"Who told you that?" Kevin swung his head toward Jackie.

"Dude, it's obvious. Plus, you asked me what I thought of her. Nobody does that unless they like someone."

Kevin reached for the bread, opened it. "She seems cool."

Taylor laughed. "You've known her for like eight years, and you're just *now* noticing?"

"I'll tell you why he just now noticed. One word…boobs," Jackie said.

Taylor's face scrunched. "Why would that matter?"

Jackie's confused look trumped Taylor's. "You serious?" He looked at Kevin. "Tell me I'm not alone here. Don't make me look like a pervert."

"Yeah, I noticed. But I don't think that's why—"

"That's exactly why. Case in point, Angie Gaurisco."

"That's because her knockers are huge," Kevin said. "*Everyone* notices them."

"Yeah. I definitely noticed those." Taylor's face relaxed.

"I think it's the natural way of things." Jackie said. "Girls grow tits, and as we get older, we want to squeeze them."

"I don't want to squeeze Angie Gaurisco's tits…or Kristy's," Taylor said.

"That's cuz you're a late bloomer." Kevin pulled two slices of bread from the loaf and set them on his lap.

"What does that even mean?" Taylor asked.

"I think he means our balls don't all drop at the same time." Jackie could barely get through the sentence before cracking up—a contagious fit that had Kevin going too. Taylor didn't laugh. "I didn't mean anything by it, Tay. It's puberty, ya know? Unpredictable and random."

Kevin spread a layer of Doritos on the bread, being careful not to break them. "My dad said never to compare ourselves with anyone else, and that we all reach manhood at different stages. Jackie's got enough hair under his arms to hide a nest of birds in, but I've got like twelve hairs. If you're not looking at tits yet, that's why. Different stages."

"So, you admit that's why you noticed Kristy?" Jackie said.

"I dunno, dude. I just think she's cool."

Taylor looked at the cover of the Penthouse, which sat on the ground next to Jackie. The model's nipples were barely covered, and her ass stuck out in an inviting manner, like it should have a sign pointing toward it.

Nothing.

A low whistling sound came from above, and the threatening, black shadows between the rows of corn filled with light. A second later, the pine trees rattled, and the earth shook as something crashed inside the pines.

"What the shovelin' shit was that?" Jackie said.

CHAPTER 14

RUNNING THROUGH THE rows at night was unsettling, worse than running up the dark basement stairs, where a pair of hands waited to grab you so you'd better haul ass and never look back. But with this run, the horror could be in front of them, like a machete waiting to clothesline their necks, yet despite the fear of running blindly through a cornfield at night and everything it could hide, nothing was going to stop them from finding out what had just crashed into the pines.

"It's a UFO," Taylor said as he ran, following the faint orange glow above the stalks, like a whole separate campfire ahead. "They exist, you know. And this is just the kind of place they'd land, an isolated place, where nobody would believe us. And the government will show up, hide it, and deny everything."

"You read too much," Jackie said from behind.

"I'll bet it's an airplane engine. You watch, tomorrow it'll be all over the news. Plane crash, three-hundred dead." Kevin still held the Dorito sandwich, his fingers buried in the bread like a handprint in freshly poured cement.

"Then where's the rest of the plane?" Jackie asked.

"Still in their air. Can you imagine? Everyone screaming, knowing they're gonna die, and then *boom*!"

As they grew closer, pushing through the darkness—the stalks slapping their arms and cutting their faces—their pace slowed to a brisk walk, then a creep. The glow was just ahead.

As they broke through the corn and hit the tree line, they saw the orange light was coming from small fires that had started in the dead needles among the trees. And there, in the middle of it all, was a large hole emitting steam.

Taylor continued his creep forward, while his friends stayed behind. For the first time in forever, he felt courageous. Maybe it had something to do with leaving home for good and the note on the fridge declaring the two words he never thought he'd say, which was a far more dangerous thing to do than approach a crashed ship full of aliens.

"Tay… get back here." Kevin whisper-yelled.

But he kept moving forward while Jackie grabbed a nearby stalk of corn like it was a comforting hand to hold.

Taylor stepped into the forest, the soft crunch of needles underfoot. The pines had always smelled so good. Sharp and fresh and almost citrusy. But now, they reeked of matches and rotten eggs, like the lingering gas that leaked from his dad while passed out in front of the TV.

A quiet hiss could be heard, but its source remained hidden, buried in the earth. A tiny dot of light through the trees caught Taylor's eye. It was Wagner's farm. He wondered if Mr. Wagner had seen the landing, or maybe even felt the crash. He pictured Mr. Wagner jumping out of bed and grabbing the nearest shotgun. While the boys were always welcome on the land, Mr. Wagner wasn't fond of trespassers and covered his property with an obscene number of signs stating so.

Taylor turned and looked at his cowardly friends, who both wore wide eyes and open mouths. He waved them forward.

"Is it aliens?" Jackie whispered.

Taylor shrugged, then turned back around.

"Wait," Kevin called out, but Taylor didn't listen. He was enjoying this new courage, this foreign thing that was long overdue.

Finally, Kevin and Jackie stepped out of the corn, away from the safety—or its many deceiving arms—of it. Between the moon and the eerie glow of fire thrown on nearby trunks and dangling branches, the scene resembled a painting meant to unsettle.

When Taylor suddenly stopped, his friends nearly ran, the Dorito sandwich in Kevin's hand now a breaded ball of shattered chips.

Taylor bent down, picked up a stick, and ran toward the hole.

Kevin and Jackie looked at each other, as though telepathically deciding on whether to follow or turn back. Then, Taylor called out to them in a voice that was shotgun loud in the ominous quiet.

"It's a meteorite!"

Kevin moved first, then Jackie, heading toward the unknown.

There, in the ground, as though it had tried to burrow, was a bumpy rock the size and shape of a large watermelon. What looked like barnacles covered the entire thing, as though floating through space had attracted otherworldly organisms hitching a ride to Earth.

In the middle of the space melon was a deep, wide fissure where ghostly steam quietly whistled out.

"It reeks," was all Kevin managed, then realized he still held the balled-up sandwich and took a bite from it.

Taylor knelt near the meteor and put the stick in the fissure, then pulled it back. A translucent goo bubbled, then solidified on the end of the stick, like cooling molten lava.

"Dude," Jackie said, stepping back. "Don't mess with it."

Taylor held the stick close to his face, then touched the hardened goo. It felt like an old globule of sap found on any given pine tree near them.

Kevin stood and watched with a mouthful of food, while Jackie gave another warning. "Dude, don't."

"It's fine." Taylor touched it again, then poked the stick into the crack once more. This time he planted his feet, putting his weight on the stick to pry the rock open. The meteor cracked, and steam hissed from its core, covering him in a noxious cloud, while the goo inside spilled and splashed, spattering his arm.

He screamed and clawed at himself while the clear napalm-like substance burned tiny holes through his flesh. Then came the coughing. His lungs grew tight, as though his stomach held a vacuum that sucked the air from his lungs, shrinking them, destroying them. It was worse than the time he tried inhaling cigarette smoke. Far worse. The coughing turned to silence as he searched for breath and his throat constricted.

Kevin and Jackie panicked, shouted, eyes glued to their suffering friend, pacing back and forth, steering clear of the cloud that lingered.

Finally, Taylor ran and caught his breath, his throat raw. He collapsed and heaved into the dirt, then crawled toward his friends, throwing himself at their feet.

"Dammit, dude. I told you," Jackie whined.

Kevin dropped his sandwich and knelt next to Taylor, who was writhing in pain, coughing. "Tay… you okay? Can you see me? Can you hear me?"

Taylor managed to bark the word, "Yes."

The cloud slowly dissipated, and the smell of pine needles afire began to replace the rotten, sulfurous odor.

Taylor sat up, looked his arm over, saw the black and red dots where the goo had splashed him. It wasn't as bad as he'd expected. After another short coughing fit, he said, "Put the fires out so the woods don't…" *Cough.* "That's all we need is the fire department to show up when we're not supposed to…" *Cough.* "Not supposed to be here."

"We might be too late," Kevin said, pointing through the woods toward Wagner's farm, where shifting beams of red and blue could be seen in the distance.

"You think Mr. Wagner heard the crash and called?" Jackie said.

"Maybe." Kevin squinted his eyes toward the farm. "Sure as hell got here fast."

"We need to get back to the fort then." *Cough.*

Kevin looked at the small fires that seemed to be dying, then the last trace of fading steam. "Yeah. Let's go."

While flashlight beams bounced in the distance, Jackie and Kevin lifted their friend and helped him walk back through the long, black hall between the corn rows, as he coughed and spat the foul taste from his mouth.

CHAPTER 15

TAYLOR LAY SHIRTLESS on the ground inside the The Pantheon II, illuminated by Jackie's lantern. His friends were outside pissing on the campfire to put it out.

Taylor gently ran his fingers over his left arm, counting the holes in his skin. Most of them were the size of a BB, with one on the inside of his forearm the size of a dime. That one hurt the most. Sixteen holes in all. None were bleeding and seemed to have cauterized themselves.

The piss-fire funk caused by Jackie and Kevin reached Taylor's nostrils, and it felt like defeat. He couldn't seem to catch a break from malodorous air, burning pain, and a sandpaper throat. He coughed, hacked, then spat on the dirt ground in the corner.

The door opened, and in came Kevin and Jackie, their faces covered in concern.

"They're at the meteor now, at least four of them," Kevin said. "I think we should go home. The place will be crawling with cops and maybe even FBI. If they make their way over here, we're screwed."

"Yeah," Jackie agreed. "Plus, you should get checked out, Tay."

Taylor coughed again, but it wasn't the harsh bark it was before. "I'm fine. It's not that bad."

"You got holes in your arm." Jackie said.

"They're not bleeding, though. Just burns. It looks worse than it is."

"We should still go. If your dad finds out—"

"I can't," Taylor said.

Kevin crouched down. "What do you mean you can't? You can't walk? Do you need an ambulance?"

"I mean I can't go home." The look on Taylor's face was as serious as they'd ever seen. It answered questions and posed more at the same time. The two studied him, making assumptions, coming to conclusions that didn't go anywhere near the actual truth.

"I left my dad a note that made sure I could never go back... even if I wanted to."

"What'd it say?" Kevin asked.

Taylor tried to smile. "It said, 'fuck you.'" This time when Taylor coughed, it was from the harsh realization of what he'd done.

Those two words were everything both friends had wanted to say to his dad for years, something they'd never said to anyone—except maybe when playing around—and certainly never to one of their own parents. But if anyone deserved a Fuck You, it was Taylor's dad.

Jackie smacked himself on the forehead with the palm of his hand.

Kevin's knees seemed to weaken, as he fell back into the beanbag chair, which barely had the cushion to break the fall comfortably. Dirt shot from under and made a small cloud around it.

"You said 'fuck you' to your *dad*?" Jackie said.

"I can't live there anymore, you guys. I just can't. I know we don't talk much about what goes on... and thanks for that... but if I stay any longer I'm afraid he'll kill me... or I'll kill him.

Taylor's words were a hammer to the face, and neither boy said a word. Suddenly, everything was different now. The Pantheon II was no longer a getaway but a necessary home, and they were all on the verge of being caught should the police wander over.

"So… what's your plan? Live here and eat Dorito sandwiches in the dark?" Kevin stood back up and paced within the small space. "It's not like you can get a job and support yourself."

"I stole a hundred bucks from my dad to live on."

"Holy shit," Jackie said. "You really *aren't* going back, are you?"

"I told you. I can't do it anymore. You don't know what it's like."

"Can't you just kiss his ass until you're like 16 and then—"

"He… he came into my room last night… when he thought I was sleeping." Taylor lifted his watery eyes toward the plywood ceiling. "He touched me."

The declaration was a blade which eviscerated every word that sat on their tongues, and silence filled the fort like the world had ceased to exist.

Kevin's eyes dropped to the ground, where they drilled holes through the dirt and projected the shameful scenario. A tsunami of guilt crashed through because of his perfect home and perfect parents and perfect bike he'd ride past his perfectly gorgeous neighbor, and because the only person who ever touched him in his bed at night was himself.

Jackie's eyes trailed out the window, into the black corn, and toward that fucking meteor that just had to come along and shit on everything, even though it had nothing to do with the real hell Taylor had been dealing with.

Taylor's eyes met the ground too, unsure if he should have revealed so much. Then, he doubled down.

"It wasn't the first time."

All eyes went to him. There didn't seem to be any other place they could have gone. Taylor needed to know he was being heard.

"I'm sorry, Tay," Kevin finally broke the fragile silence.

"Me too." Jackie scooted toward him and put a reassuring hand on his shoulder.

"Fuck him, right?" Taylor said.

"Fuck him." A unified chorus of two that brought the corner of Taylor's mouth up—the hint of a smile that never fully blossomed.

"If my mom were still alive, I'll bet she'd take me away and leave his ass."

"Hell yeah, she would, Tay," Jackie said.

The fort filled with dreadful silence, and every word said in the past few minutes seemed to bounce off the walls, ricocheting, looping through their minds and solidifying itself in their memories.

Finally, Jackie grabbed a pontoon cushion and spread out a blanket on the dirt floor. "Well, I guess if we're gonna get caught tonight, we may as well stick together,"

Kevin did the same. "I'm in."

"Are you really feeling better, Tay?" Jackie asked.

"My arm is sore is all."

"How long do you think they'll be out there?" Jackie looked up at the window and the stars beyond.

"All night. They'll bring in experts. Scientists and agents and photographers, probably tie off the area like it's some crime scene." Taylor shifted his arm, trying to get it into a comfortable position. If it weren't for the larger spot on the inside of his forearm, it'd be easier.

"We should turn the lantern off." Kevin's eyes were on the poster, using the image to escape and file away.

Jackie leaned over and shut the lantern off. "What do you think they'll do with the meteor?"

"Maybe we should have stayed there. It could be worth a lot of money. Like, what if a museum buys it for a million dollars?" Kevin said.

"The money would probably go to Mr. Wagner," Jackie said.

Taylor chuckled. "I don't think it's worth a million dollars. They'll probably run tests on it, keep it in a lab somewhere for research."

There was a moment of silence while heads filled with speculation—thoughts on being a millionaire and everything that could be purchased with the money. Then the discussion trailed back to the traumatic event.

"Did it feel like a regular burn?" Jackie said. "Like when you burn your hand on the stove?"

"Sort of, but it lasted longer, like it wouldn't stop."

"Oh, man. What if it was like in that movie *Alien*, where its blood was acid and ate through your whole arm and didn't stop until it was three feet in the ground."

"Then it would have eaten through the meteor on its way here," Kevin said.

"It didn't eat through the alien."

"That was a movie."

Taylor managed to ignore the pain and let the smile happen, as he drifted off to sleep while listening to the banter of his best friends by his side.

CHAPTER 16

KEVIN WOKE AT 4:00 a.m. with a bladder full of Mountain Dew. He crept outside, careful not to wake the others. He looked toward the tree line. Over the towering corn, it was like daylight at the meteor site. Fluorescent light shot through the tree limbs. The scientists and cops and federal agents—and maybe even Mr. Wagner—were still there, doing whatever it is they do when a goo-filled meteor hits the earth. And even though he didn't want those people anywhere near the fort, it was somehow comforting to know they were near, almost in the same way the light that spilled from his garage was.

He walked one corn row over and pissed on the ground. They'd made a rule to never pee so close to the fort, but when the rule was made, they hadn't considered the dark, and no way was he heading out further. If they can deal with the smell of otherworldly egg and campfire piss, they can deal with piss-dirt too.

After relieving himself, he went back inside the fort and curled up on the blanket, eyes open. He missed the comfort of his bed, his pillow. And the idea of sleeping out here in the field on the hard ground while worrying whether or not your parents would find out was certainly an idea that looked better on paper. This would most likely be the last time they'd do this, except for Taylor.

Kevin turned toward his friend, who slept on his stomach, arms at his sides. The moon seemed to be shining more on him than anywhere else, like a pale-skinned ginger in a line of tanned sunbathers. Kevin sat up, looked at Jackie, looked at Taylor. *Was* it the moon? Or was he really that pale?

He watched him carefully, looking for the rise of lungs being filled, listening for a quiet breath.

Nothing.

He scooted closer. Watched. Listened. He wanted to place a hand on his back or fingers on his wrist to feel for a pulse like they did in the movies, but he dare not haunt his friend's sleep with an unexpected touch.

Finally, Taylor stirred, turned on his side, and offered a deep sigh. Kevin collapsed with relief, closed his eyes, and tried not to think about that pale skin in the moonlight.

CHAPTER 17

TAYLOR WOKE FIRST. He peeled his lids open and was greeted by the tits that seemed to haunt him now. He felt okay. His throat was still a little scratchy, but his arm didn't burn like it had last night.

Birds chirped from somewhere nearby, and sunlight lit the fort in a way he hadn't seen before, offering a warm orange hue that covered the walls inside. It dawned on him they'd never been at the fort this early in the morning. It was pleasant. Uplifting.

He turned his head, saw his friends, and smiled. They'd stuck it out, stayed with him. The most loyal friends ever.

He went to sit up but struggled. Something wasn't allowing it. He tried again and fell on his side in pain. That's when he found the culprit: His left arm. It was stuck, as though welded along his ribs and across his stomach. The more he tried to move it, the worse the pain was, like what it might feel like to rip the webbing between your fingers, or the corners of your mouth by opening your jaw too wide. The splitting of flesh.

Finally, using his right arm only, he sat up and inspected the dead limb. The burn holes seemed to have sealed on their own with a thin membrane, not quite healed but not the angry red they were the night before.

It was at this point Taylor realized the bitter taste still lingered. But it was more than that. It was the feel of his tongue and how it sat in his mouth, as though the muscle had died and merely lounged like putty between his teeth, the flesh seeping into every open crevice.

He panicked, then shouted, "Can I still talk?" His voice sounded like it always had. No lisp. No lazy tongue.

Jackie stirred and mumbled.

Kevin shot up onto his elbows. "What, dude?"

Taylor stalled, unsure of what to say, then: "I was just saying we made it. No cops. No feds." He sat up as naturally as he could, making sure his immobile arm was hidden.

"Ohh… Yeah, cool." Kevin laid back down and rubbed the sleep from his eyes. "I'm starving. Any of those chips left?"

Taylor eyed the chips in the corner next to the bread. There looked to be some in there, but if he got up, Kevin would see his arm and freak, telling him he needed a doctor. And that would involve his dad, which would involve a beating, and if he didn't die from the beating, well…

"Not sure," he said. "While you're up, grab me the Dew."

"How's your throat?"

"Good as new."

"And your arm?"

"Much better. Doesn't even hurt anymore." He scooted toward the bench and leaned back, grabbed the blanket, and covered himself.

"Cold?" Kevin asked him.

"A little."

Finally, Jackie sat up, squinted. "I slept like shit. Dreamt about aliens all night. It doesn't even feel real. A fucking meteor, you guys."

Kevin laughed, and Taylor faked it.

"Think they're still there?" Jackie sat up, pulled at his shirt, making sure his belly was covered.

"Probably. What time is it, Tay?"

Without thinking, Taylor went to check his watch and grimaced at the effort. What the hell was going on?

"My watch died. It's probably 6:00, maybe 7:00."

"So, what's for breakfast?" Jackie said, reaching for a 2-liter.

"Oh, let's see. Doritos over easy, scrambled, or au gratin." Kevin crawled over Taylor's legs, reached for the bag of chips. "Or how about croutons? Someone left the bread open. Gonna be stale as shit."

"You sound like my mom," Jackie said.

"I think I did that," Taylor said. "Sorry."

"No biggie." Kevin grabbed the other 2 liter and set it on Taylor's lap.

"Thanks."

No way Taylor could open the pop and drink from it without them noticing the awkwardness of using one arm to do it. He picked it up and set it next to him, his throat drier than ever, his tongue a puddle of gum that'd been chewed for too long.

He wanted them to leave so he could figure things out, pull the arm from his side and scream. It felt like that's what it would take, lots of screaming.

"Let's address the elephant in the room, guys. What are you doin', Tay?" Jackie took a swig from his 2-liter.

"What do you mean?" Taylor asked.

"Like, are you gonna head into town and get food and stuff, or are you going… what's the word I'm lookin' for?"

"Incognito?" Kevin offered.

"Yeah, I think that's it. Are you gonna be incognito? We can get you supplies if that's what you're gonna do. Incognito, or whatever."

Taylor knew that wasn't really the word Jackie was looking for, but it was close enough.

"Yeah, I'm gonna stay here. I don't wanna run into my dad or anyone who knows him."

"Save your money for now," Kevin said. "We'll grab you some stuff from home."

"I got a book you can read," Jackie said. "I'll never read it. Shit, you can have it."

"I've got one in my bag, thanks. Maybe you could go right now and get some stuff? I was thinking about going back to bed. I didn't sleep so good, either."

Jackie and Kevin traded glances.

"Sure, okay." Kevin grabbed his shoes. "You want some cough drops?"

"Yeah. And maybe some Tylenol."

"I'll hook you up with some more chips," Jackie said.

"He can't live off junk food," Kevin said.

"I know." Jackie tugged at his shirt. "I just mean for a snack. I'll grab some apples and carrots too."

"Thanks, guys." Taylor wanted to say more. He wanted to tell them he was scared to death and they had no idea how thankful he is to have them as friends. But the words wouldn't come because they just didn't talk like that. Maybe when they're older. Maybe if shit gets so bad there's no choice but to use words like that because they're the only thing that can save you.

"I got chores. So, how about we meet back here after lunch?" Kevin grabbed his backpack and stood up.

"You guys." Taylor said. "Promise me you won't tell anyone I'm here."

"Why would we do that?" Kevin said.

"My dad can't know. Nobody can. Okay?"

"Yeah, we know."

"Promise me." The desperation on Taylor's face was almost frightening, and though somewhat confused, both boys promised.

"Make the oath. And if you tell anyone, you drink the piss."

"We're not gonna say anything, Tay. Don't worry." Jackie said.

"Make the oath." Taylor spit on his hand and held it out. His friends did the same. Then they all joined hands in a triangle of unity that meant serious business, a handshake first invented when they'd made the promise to always stick up for the other if Kip Lennon ever started shit with them the way he did the computer geeks at school.

With stone-set faces, the boys nodded at each other, solidifying the deal.

"Okay, now get some sleep." Kevin opened the door, and the morning light shot through, forcing Taylor's eyes shut.

"See ya soon, dude." Jackie followed Kevin out the door.

Taylor listened to the slapping of cornstalk leaves against limbs, until the sound faded. He ripped the blanket off his body and looked at his left side, terrified to attempt any sort of movement.

He used his right arm to try and pull the left from his side, and the stinging pain was unbearable. It was as though his arm was never meant to be anything more than a growth on his side that should never be touched, let alone torn away.

With one hand, he uncapped the Mountain Dew and drank like a fiend in the desert. His tongue felt detached, as though at any moment it would slide down his throat and settle in his belly. The carbonation burned his throat, and the bubbles flew north and out his nose in a snot-filled burp that sprayed like a thumb at the end of a hose.

He set the pop between his legs and capped it, then wiped his face with the blanket. With his one good arm, Taylor braced himself on the bench, then stood up. When he opened the door of the fort, the sun seemed impossibly bright. This was more than just waiting until your eyes acclimated. This was like the time his mom took him to the eye doctor, when they put the drops in his eyes to dilate them. They made him wear those funny-looking sunglasses. And when his dad saw him, he said he looked like a faggot, like that fella who sang, *Goodbye Yellow Brick Road.*

Taylor walked ten rows from the fort—according to the Pantheon II rules—and peed between the stalks.

He looked down at his arm. In the light, he could clearly see the seam where the skin of his arm met his ribs and stomach, like it'd been stitched there and covered in wax. He gently pulled at it. The skin there lifted and stretched, then the pain came back.

His heart raced, and his breathing intensified as panic set in. This was a nightmare. Had to be. He ran back to the fort, grabbed his notebook and pen and with his good arm began to write, doing what he could to escape and keep from hyperventilating.

CHAPTER 18

THE NEXT DAY, *after the beast brought the usual bowl of gruel, the boy ate none of it. As hungry as he was, he couldn't afford to use the food for anything but his plan for escape. Even if it meant starving.*

The dark, dank prison had taken hold of his mind, and he sensed the pull of turning into a monster himself, of giving into the insanity that poked at him. And he knew if he didn't kill the beast himself or escape these prison walls, his days were numbered. The beast had grown angrier with each visit, perhaps even hungry for the boy's flesh. It would only be a matter of time.

He applied the entire bowl of gruel to the outside of three of the bars. It was sure to dry like cement, just like it had before.

The sun beamed down with a scorching ferocity as though it meant to destroy every living thing. Not a cloud in the sky.

Perfect.

CHAPTER 19

WHEN KEVIN AND Jackie returned, Taylor was sound asleep, drained from unrelenting anxiety as well as the heat. He had managed to take his shorts off and cover himself with a blanket, which had since slipped off, hiding nothing.

Jackie saw it first.

Had it only been Taylor's arm seemingly resting at his side, it could have been overlooked. But it was his hand that drew attention, which now resembled a flipper more than four fingers and a thumb. Taylor's fingers had melded together in a seamless paddle of flesh, while the skin on the rest of his arm seemed to be slowly creeping toward its new home on his ribs and belly, like a stick of butter melting in the sun, becoming one with his torso.

"Oh my God!"

Kevin followed Jackie's wide eyes, leaned in, and tried to make sense of the deformity. He dropped to his knees, grabbed Taylor's shoulder, and shook him. "Tay! Wake up!"

Taylor's eyes flew open. Panicked, he went for the blanket with his other hand. His body contorted, and he screamed in pain.

Kevin jumped back, afraid he'd hurt him, unsure of what to do. "Tay, what happened?"

"I'm gettin' Wagner," Jackie said and turned toward the door.

"No!" Taylor called out. "You promised."

"Dude, something's wrong with you. We have to." Kevin said.

"We made an oath. Do you want me to fucking die?!"

"No, we don't. That's exactly why we have to tell someone." Jackie stood with his hand on the door.

"I knew you'd do this."

"Wait...how long have you been like this?" Kevin asked.

"Since this morning, when I woke up." Taylor looked down and saw the unspeakable mess of progression. "Oh shit!" He struggled to sit up, moving the free half of his body, almost resembling an insect that'd been smacked and left for dead, dragging its useless limbs as it crawled in an endless circle.

Jackie ran to his side, where he and Kevin helped sit him up, being careful not to touch the mutilated side.

Kevin sat on the ground next to him. "What even happened? I mean...how—"

"Bet it was the meteor," Jackie said. "That shit got all over you, and you breathed it. It's like that one movie with the—"

"You guys, I know this looks bad, but I'm not going to the doctor, and I'm not going to the hospital. And if you tell anyone, not only will you be drinking the piss, but you won't have me as a friend." Taylor pulled the blanket back over his arm. With its ornamental filigree pattern, the blanket resembled the single wing of a Monarch butterfly.

"That's not fair," Jackie said. "You'd do the same for us. You'd get help."

"Yeah," Kevin said.

"If you knew everything, you'd never tell. You'd *never* let that asshole near me again." Taylor buried his face into his hand, and his body trembled.

With everything Taylor had been through, from losing his mother to the abuse from his father, no one had ever seen him cry, not even a quivering chin, though he'd been given every reason to. Instead, every tear that should have been shed was kept inside. Taylor Singletree was a sponge, absorbing the tears, the punches and the kicks, the words from his father's forked tongue, the grief, and the trauma. But now the sponge was full and could hold no more.

Jackie knelt on the other side of his friend. "We know you don't like to talk about it, so I guess we just wanted to…what's the word?"

"Respect?" Kevin said.

"Yeah, we just wanted to respect that. But you can tell us anything, dude."

Taylor pinched the bridge of his nose and wiped the tears away. He looked at Jackie, then at Kevin. Their faces were filled with sincerity. He sighed, then took a deep breath. "He killed my mom."

"Your dad did?" Kevin said.

Jackie dropped on his butt and pulled his shirt out from any fold it may have tucked into.

"Yeah." Taylor shifted, tried his best to get comfortable, but it wasn't working. So, he had his friends prop him up in the corner against his pillow and a few of the pontoon cushions. "I saw some letters he wrote, like apologies to her… confessions. But before that, one night he came into my room, drunk, and sat on my bed. He didn't know I was awake, and he started crying and apologizing to me for Mom dying, saying it was his fault. At first, I thought he just felt guilty, like maybe he thought there was something he could have done to save her from drowning, but when I read the letters, it all made sense. He killed her. He fucking killed her."

The boys sat stunned, staring off like they were reading something shocking written on the walls.

"Why didn't you…" Jackie seemed to choose his words carefully. "Why didn't you tell the police?"

"I wanted to, but you know how they are. It's like a roll of the dice sometimes. And the lawyers on them TV shows are always pulling stuff outta their ass to make things go away, even if they know the guy did it. Unless I was sure he was gonna go to jail, I couldn't say a word. He'd kill me. No doubt about it."

Kevin stood up. "We gotta do something. That guy belongs in prison." Kevin started pacing, three steps this way, spin, three steps that way. "Fucking pervert murderer, ass-beatin' cocksucker."

The word pervert seemed to echo. Even though Taylor had given them an idea of what his dad had done, it was still cryptic. No questions were asked, and no details given, but that word felt like salt in a wound that was so fresh, Taylor hadn't had much time to process just exactly what in the fuck his dad was thinking or why he'd do such a thing to his own son.

Finally, Kevin stopped pacing and looked straight at Taylor. "This might sound gay…but I don't care. I love you, Tay. We'll do whatever you want. If you want us to walk up there right now and take a baseball bat to his face, we will."

Jackie looked up at Kevin. "We will?"

"Hell yes."

"Okay… just checkin."

"Or if you want us to leave things be while you heal up and figure shit out, we'll do that too."

Taylor smiled, and it was genuine, despite the fear. "We'll figure it out."

"Yes, we will. And you'll be done with this bullshit. We'll make sure of it. Right, Jackie?"

"Yeah." Jackie wiped sweat from his lip that didn't seem to be accumulating on anyone else's. "We'll make sure of it."

"How are the burns? And how's your throat?"

"My throat doesn't really hurt anymore. It just feels...weird. So does my tongue. But the burns are kinda healed up already."

"You know what?" Jackie said, looking at Taylor's arm. "Maybe you've got superpowers, like when Spiderman got bit by the radio spider—"

"Radioactive."

"Radioactive spider, and Bruce Banner with the gamma stuff. Maybe something cool will come out of this. There's a big universe out there. Lots of stuff we don't know about. Maybe that meteor with its stuff inside is something good."

All three of them looked at Taylor's flipper-hand.

Taylor frowned and shrugged with his right shoulder. "Maybe."

"Hey!" Kevin reached for his backpack. "We brought stuff."

Jackie grabbed his bag too and the boys took turns unloading them, excitedly revealing the things they'd brought from home, lining them up for display: Half a frozen pizza that had been cooked then wrapped in tinfoil, a milk jug full of water, another 2-liter of Mountain Dew, an old can opener, cans of corn, baked beans, and tuna, a package of hot dog buns, peanut butter, a butter knife, two apples, three carrots, and two hard-boiled eggs, one of which was crushed.

"Wow. Thanks for the rations, guys. That'll do for a while."

"Maybe we could plant a little garden, and you could live off the land," Jackie said.

"Might be too late in the year for that," Kevin said.

"Not for carrots. We could plant those." Taylor seemed excited at the prospect. Roughing it, tending to a garden, maybe even expanding on the fort and adding another room.

The three of them talked excitedly about the idea of expanding and decided that's exactly what they'd do, build Taylor his own bedroom and this would be the living room. They even talked about having an underground bunker fortified with railroad ties and how it could be a shelter from future meteor storms and a true hideout where if someone did discover the fort (like the police or, God forbid, Taylor's dad) no one would ever be able to find the secret hidden bunker.

Then Taylor grimaced and doubled over. "Did you bring the Tylenol?"

"Shit. Almost forgot. Cough drops too…" Jackie reached in his pocket and pulled out a plastic baggie filled with 12 loose pills and eight individually wrapped honey-lemon cough drops. "Here you go. I'll get the water." He grabbed the milk jug and set it next to Taylor. "Not sure if you're supposed to take one or two. My mom still has me take the kid's stuff."

Taylor opened the baggie and grabbed two.

The excitement of expanding the fort had died down, and darkness seemed to fill the place, like a cloud overhead meant to remind them they were having far too much fun and should be ashamed.

"Have you guys been to the meteor?" Taylor asked, popping the pills in his mouth.

Both boys said they hadn't and weren't even sure if anyone was still there.

"You need anything else?" Kevin asked.

Taylor shook his head.

"I know you don't want us to say anything, but if you change your mi—"

"I'm not gonna change my mind." Taylor glowered at Kevin. "I'd rather die here than give my dad the satisfaction."

"You're not gonna die here."

"Hell no you're not," Jackie said.

Kevin patted Taylor on the shoulder. "Jackie's gonna stay, but I've got ball practice, and my dad's taking us out for ice cream after."

Jackie glared at Kevin for the mention of ice cream and dads that gave a shit.

"But we probably won't end up getting ice cream. He just says that sometimes." It was a lie. Kevin's dad was the poster boy for exemplary fathers, and everyone knew it.

"My mom wants me to do some chores later, but she's got her face buried in a book, so I can hang out until close to dinner. Maybe we can draw up some blueprints for the additions."

"What's she reading?" Taylor asked.

"A horror book. One of them ones that have the window on the cover with a scary face behind it."

"Does she read Clive Barker?"

"I dunno, probably. I don't pay much attention."

"She should read Clive Barker. He's the best. Grab that book inside the bench, will you?"

While Jackie got the book, Kevin said goodbye and promised to be back in the morning. "I'll bring a shovel, and we'll start the bunker."

Taylor offered a half smile and watched Kevin shut the door behind him..

"Damn…this looks awesome!" Jackie handed the pristine hardcover copy of *The Thief of Always* to Taylor.

"Been saving it for a special occasion," Taylor said. But it didn't feel like a special occasion at all. It felt like the only occasion left.

CHAPTER 20

JACKIE SPENT THE rest of the afternoon with Taylor. They managed to no longer speak of the obvious and instead talked more about the fort and aliens and whether or not space visitors are something they should fear. But mostly they talked about books.

"Will you read it?" Taylor held up his book.

"Yeah, sure."

"I mean…right now. Out loud."

"Oh." Jackie pulled at his shirt. "I'm not that great with…what's the word? Like when you sound stuff out?"

"Pronunciation."

"Yeah, I'm not good with that sometimes."

"It's not a hard book. Not like what your mom reads. Clive wrote this one for us."

Jackie took the book, looked it over, studied the wild artwork for the third time, then opened it up and turned to chapter one, reading the first paragraph to himself. "Out loud, huh?"

"Yeah." Taylor smiled with anticipation, but it fell to a thin line as he struggled to get comfortable. Sitting up stretched his arm, and he could only lean on his right side for so long before becoming restless. He could lie down completely with his legs slightly bent so it didn't stretch the fused skin, but it made him think of being a baby in a crib, his mother reading a bedtime story.

"Never mind. I'll read it." Taylor held his hand out for the book.

"You sure?"

"Yes, I'm sure. I'm not a baby."

"Huh?"

"Just give me the book. I'll read it."

Jackie handed the book over, then sat and listened to his friend read until Taylor started pausing every so often. Finally, Jackie realized Taylor had been dosing off.

"Hey," he said. "It's dinner time. You want a sandwich?"

Taylor did his best to sit upright, pretending he wasn't that tired. "Not hungry, thanks. You should get going. Your mom is probably expecting you about now."

"Yeah. Sorry, dude."

"Don't be. Thanks for hanging out."

Jackie's brow furrowed. "You're my friend, Tay. Of course. It's just like any other day, right?"

"Right."

But it wasn't like any other day. When Jackie closed the door and the sound of slapping cornstalks faded, Taylor wept harder than he ever had in his entire life. It wasn't like any other day at all.

CHAPTER 21

FINALLY, AFTER FAR *too many years in the prison, there was hope. The sun had dried the thick clumps of gruel onto the bars, and all that was left was the wait, and to pray that the beast would never poke his grotesque head in and spot with his yellow eyes the plan for escape the boy had set in motion.*

For hours he waited, watching through the window. When nothing happened, he began to caw, doing his best imitation of the large birds he'd seen outside for so many years. It was the only language he spoke anymore.

When two birds approached, it felt surreal, like winged angels sent by God. He slowly backed away from the window and sat on the dirty floor as the birds ferociously pecked away with their giant beaks at the cement-like gruel adhered to the bars.

But then, the thundering footsteps of the beast approaching shook the cell and frightened the birds away. The chain rattled and the lock fell. But what scared the boy most was that it wasn't even time for dinner.

CHAPTER 22

JUST BEFORE DARK, Taylor went outside and walked ten rows away, pulled his shorts down and did his best to squat between the rows. With some maneuvering and awkward positioning of his left leg, he managed a bowel movement, then stood and wiped with the widest leaf he could find from the surrounding stalks. The leaf was like a brittle cat's tongue across his rectum, and he made a mental note about needing to get toilet paper, or at least next time bring a page from the Penthouse, maybe one of the articles so as not to steal the joy away from his friends.

He stared at the sky—his arm plastered to his side, his fingers gone—and looked for signs of life, maybe a spaceship hovering over, monitoring his progress after the meteor's noxious attack, waiting for the right moment to come and save him—an otherworldly good Samaritan who could no longer stand idly by and watch the suffering of a 12-year-old boy.

But the sky was still and barren. The stars had not yet been given permission by the sun to boast their numbers, and the moon hid somewhere, waiting its turn.

Taylor's legs grew weak, and he set off toward the fort. He smiled at the ridiculous punishment of piss that stood upright on the roof like some threatening gargoyle, not really to protect but to remind the three of them that oaths were not to be broken.

After folding, then stacking the blankets into a makeshift mattress, Taylor made himself as comfortable as his body allowed, then grabbed his book and fell asleep before finishing the page he was on.

CHAPTER 23

KEVIN AND JACKIE parked their bikes in the pines and began their walk down the thirteenth row. The sky was overcast, thick and gray, like it should have been raining by now.

Kevin held a folded local newspaper in one hand. The front page had an article about the meteor that seemed to make light of the discovery and gave no indication as to where it was found. The article was vague and almost cryptic, adding to their already conspiratorial stance on the government and its untold discovery of UFOs, aliens, and even falling bits from space. As promised, Kevin had also brought a shovel to begin construction on the bunker.

"I feel like we need to do something about his dad," Jackie said, patting the stalks with his hand as they passed them by.

"Me too, but what?"

"I say we get them letters Tay was talking about and show them to the police."

"You mean like, break into the house?"

"We'd have to. It's not like he'd just hand them over." Jackie jumped in the air and hawked a loogie, clearing three rows of corn.

"You know how easy it'd be? He's never home, and when he is, he's passed out drunk. We'd be in and out."

Kevin stopped walking and stuck his arm out to stop Jackie, catching him in the belly and causing a chain reaction of shirt tugging. First the right side, then the left. "Are you being serious? Rick Fields got caught breaking into the old gas station on 20th and went to juvie."

"That's because he's a dumbass. We won't get caught."

"But if we did, he probably wouldn't even call the cops. He'd deal with us himself, drown us like he did Mrs. Singletree."

"Or beat us to death." Jackie shook his head like he was trying to rid his mind of the entire scenario. "But we wouldn't get caught."

Kevin started walking again. "No way. I'm not doing it."

Jackie followed. "We'd be like fugilantes."

"Vigilantes. But no way. We're not doing it. One of these days, someone will figure it out, and he'll end up behind bars."

"If that were true, they woulda by now."

"We're twelve, Jackie. We ain't even had sex yet. Shit, you ain't even seen a boob outside of that magazine."

"Just cause you saw Ms. Neil's tits don't mean you're any closer to sex than I am."

"No, but I got more experience. I know what real breasts look like."

Jackie seemed to tire of the argument and kept quiet, going back to slapping the cornstalks with his hand.

"Sorry, Jackie. I just don't wanna get caught, okay?"

"Yeah, I get it."

Kevin stuck the shovel in the ground outside the fort, then opened the door. Taylor was on the floor, covered with a blanket. The only thing exposed was his good arm poking out from beneath. His book was next to him. It reminded Kevin too much of a crime scene. It didn't look good.

Like checking for a pulse from afar, Kevin called out with a cracked voice that came more from distress than puberty. "Tay!"

"Hmmm." Taylor mumbled, followed by a heavy wheeze.

"Wake up, sleepyhead. Time to get the bunker started." The enthusiasm in Kevin's voice was made of brittle plastic.

Taylor stirred.

"Brought you some cookies." Jackie held up a large Ziploc bag. "Homemade chocolate chip."

Kevin plopped down in the beanbag chair. Jackie set the cookies on the bench, grabbed a pontoon cushion, and sat on the ground.

"Feelin' any better?" Kevin wanted to pull back the blanket and feel the cool sense of relief at the sight of his friend with his arm back, good as new. But the blanket was like a death shroud he was afraid hid something worse.

"Go away," The way Taylor said it was unsettling—a smothered voice and frozen lips. Something was very wrong.

Jackie and Kevin looked at each other, then Jackie reached over and did what Kevin couldn't, pulled the cover from their friend's head.

He gasped and flinched back. "Oh God! No no no…" His voice was a ghost at midnight, instilling the terror of a thousand nightmares to come.

Kevin wouldn't look. He couldn't bear to see anything but progress, healing. He launched from the beanbag, ran outside, and kept running, toward the pines, toward the meteor site. The cornstalk's sharp leaves reached out for him, slicing his arms as though trying to stop his escape, taunting him with their smacking whispers—a green hallway a million miles long that clawed at the memories he'd made and now threatened to erode, creating scars that would run too deep for a young boy's mind to sustain.

He reached the end of the field and heaved, head spinning. He looked to his left, and there within the trees was the site. It'd been taped off. Piles of dirt sat in mounds surrounding the hole like freshly packed graves. No one was around.

He ran through the pines and broke through the tape. As suspected, the meteor was gone. This was the dirty aftermath of a scientific one-night stand. A gangbang of men had dug the earth, studied, and collected, leaving their trace behind.

Kevin knelt by the vacant hole. The beginning of the end.

He wanted to pray but wasn't sure to whom… or what. He wanted to know that whatever allowed this horrible thing to happen could hear his pleas and offer help, revealing a secret antidote he could use to bring Taylor back to normal. A potion made of herbs and berries he could concoct. Or maybe magic words he could recite that would reverse the curse, and the past few days would be nothing more than a crazy story to tell around a million campfires together.

Raising his face toward the ceiling of trees, he pleaded. "If something can hear me, and you can help…please do it." His unsteady voice rang through the empty forest. "He doesn't deserve this. He's already dealt with so much. All he wants to do is write stories. And if you help him, this'll be a great one to tell." Tears left white streaks through the thin layer of dirt on his face. "Just think about it, okay? It'd be a good one, the story. Just let him write it. Let him write a happy ending… one where he's okay and his dad doesn't mess with him ever again." He wiped the tears away, creating a streak of salty mud. "Well… that's it. I hope you heard me." He ripped a handful of needles from the ground, threw them, then buried his face in his hands and wept.

CHAPTER 24

JACKIE STARED AT his friend, who stared back with one eye. The other had been smoothed over by Taylor's own flesh. The left side of his mouth drooped downward, the corner of it sealed shut. Taylor Singletree was melding together.

Taylor's hair was filled with sweat, streaked across his forehead. The one eye bubbled with tears, glistening like that painting Jackie's mother had of the wide-eyed cat in the trash-filled alley. Until today, he liked that painting.

"Are you hot?" Jackie said.

Taylor nodded, and the tear fell.

"I'm gonna take your blanket off, okay?"

Another nod.

Jackie carefully pulled the blanket off his friend, revealing more and more of the transformation. Taylor's arm was nothing more than a long, protruding mound of flesh that followed his side and lay flat and wide across his stomach, his hand completely buried within. The boy's underwear seemed to be dissolving into a piss-stained membrane that covered his genitals. Both legs were fused together, with the seam between them disappearing. As a whole,

Taylor resembled a human candle left in the sun—skin like wax, as though you could smooth out any blemish or bump with a warm hand. But his right arm still remained free and mobile, making him appear as though he were emerging from a giant cocoon.

"I'm so sorry, Tay." Jackie's voice was a broken rattle. His face scrunched, and his eyes welled with tears. Other than those few consoling words, Jackie was speechless. He wanted to run like Kevin had and bury his head in the sand, pour bleach on the memory of his friend writhing like a maggot in the middle of a cornfield.

"What...what can I do, Tay?"

Taylor squirmed on the mattress he'd made, and saliva dripped from the side of his mouth, collecting in a pool that had started hours ago. "Water," he managed.

Jackie grabbed the milk jug. Realizing Taylor couldn't sit up, he filled the jug lid, put it to the open side of Taylor's mouth, and poured. He caught most of it, and Jackie repeated the process until Taylor shook his head, indicating no more.

Then, the fort door opened.

CHAPTER 25

KEVIN PEEKED IN, saw Taylor, and gasped, covering his mouth. He stood there at the threshold like a frightened toddler at the foot of a funhouse. Bloodshot eyes big as plums. When Taylor looked at him with his one eye, Kevin looked away and grabbed his stomach.

"I gotta sit down," he managed, then his knees gave out and he dropped, catching himself before his head hit the ground.

"He's just worried about you is all, Tay. You're doing fine." It was an outrageous lie. He wanted to throw the blanket back over him and hide the proof that he wasn't fine at all, but Taylor was covered in sweat, shiny like a clam fresh from its shell.

Once Kevin collected himself, he sat in the corner and stared, entranced by the horrendous transmogrification. It was clear that even if they broke the sacred oath and told the whole world right now, nothing could be done. The damage was otherworldly, and no medicine on Earth could tackle such a rapid breakdown of the human body. And if Kevin was truly honest with himself, it was cruel to even wish that Taylor breathed another day. This wasn't the beginning of the end. This *was* the end.

As Kevin gazed at the waxy gleam of his friend's pale flesh, hatred brewed within him. This was Taylor's dad's fault. They would have gone to the hospital immediately after finding the meteor, and Taylor would have agreed, and maybe whatever had infected or poisoned or infested him would have been cast out and cured, and blueprints would be drawn of their big future plans, maybe even for a second floor if they found themselves determined enough. And the vault of memories they'd held so dear would feel empty in comparison to how many more there were to come. But that murdering piece of shit took it all away.

"Tay, where are those letters your dad wrote?" Kevin's face was made of stone.

Taylor shifted the vulture eye over at Kevin, and through a raspy wheeze asked, "Why?"

"Because that fucker's going to prison."

There was new life behind Jackie's eyes at Kevin's statement.

"Don't want… you… in trouble." Taylor managed. So many words in succession sounded painful and strenuous to muster.

"I won't get caught. I promise. And I keep my promises. You know that."

As Taylor closed his eye, it rolled back first, and it was hard to tell if the motion was disapproval, consideration, or if that was the end, his melting body finally succumbing to the throes of death.

"Tay?"

The eye opened. "Closet." Then closed again.

Kevin shot up from the ground. "Wait here, Jackie."

"Now?" Jackie asked, but Kevin was already out the door, and the fading slap of cornstalk leaves gone within seconds.

CHAPTER 26

THERE WERE TWO ways this could be done. At night, when it was dark, and the man was at the bar or passed out drunk. Or in the middle of the day while he was at work. Kevin's rage made the decision for him. Plus, he knew if he waited, he'd go back to his original stance on the idea.

He rode down Peck Street toward Taylor's house. His was the overgrown mess at the end, which made for the perfect location for a B and E in broad daylight.

Kevin hadn't thought to ask Taylor the best way into the house. He was too filled with ire. Not to mention he was afraid Taylor would talk him out of it. Or make him promise not to.

Approaching the driveway seemed to cool Kevin's temper, the anger turning to dread. This was no rage-fueled fantasy anymore. This was the real deal.

He dumped his bike in a small group of trees thick with foliage just behind the mailbox, then walked up the driveway. Jacob Singletree's rusted Impala was gone—a car that seemed to make everyone in town cringe at the sight of it, with its primered gray door and taillight held together with tape.

When Taylor's mom had died, there was an insurance policy, but that went quick. Most of it was lost at the casino, and rumor had it that cocaine and prostitutes were no strangers to the man's short-lived fast-lane lifestyle at the time. Taylor saw none of that money, save for a used bike from a garage sale barely worth the twenty-dollar price tag.

Kevin checked the front doormat first. No key. He tried the knob. Locked. Behind the house was a screened-in porch cluttered with junk—boxes, tools, a motorcycle frame, a cinder-block end-table with a Hustler magazine spread facedown, three empty beer bottles—one of which had a candle stuck through the top—and a lighter with a picture of a large-mouth bass on the side.

He opened the screen door and passed through the maze of junk, gripped the knob on the back door. Locked.

Two feet to the right was a dirty window that led to the kitchen. He could tell from where he stood the window was unlocked. He pulled it open, then looked behind him at nothing but a mostly-dirt yard, a woodpile, and trees and brush blocking any other house nearby.

Going foot first, Kevin broke into the Singletree house.

CHAPTER 27

JACKIE READ FROM *The Thief of Always* while Taylor wheezed. At times, the wheeze turned into a whistle, startling Jackie, and he swore the open space between Taylor's lips was getting smaller. Before long, his mouth would close. And then what? Would his nostrils too? Or had they already, deep inside?

"Are you enjoying the book?"

Taylor nodded.

"Maybe you should talk more, Tay. I'm afraid your mouth will—"

"Yesthh." With the word came spittle. And fear. His mouth was most definitely getting smaller.

Taylor reached for his notebook and pen and began to write. The words were legible but shaky.

Can't live like this

He tapped the notebook to make sure Jackie read it.

Jackie sighed. "I don't know what to do, Tay. Tell me what to do. I'll do anything." He tried hard to hold back tears but failed.

When Taylor heard the whimpering and saw Jackie's wrinkled face, the wheeze-whistling picked up, and his body jerked in spasms, while his eye went thick with tears.

"We…we need to get you help, Tay. Please let us."

Taylor scribbled furiously on the notebook, underlining the word NO several times, then pushed the notebook away and gave Jackie a quivering, stern look.

Jackie lunged at his friend and hugged him, paying no mind as to whether or not it hurt.

Taylor wrapped his one arm around Jackie, and the two trembled and bawled together, creating perhaps the last memory they'd ever share.

CHAPTER 28

KEVIN RAN THROUGH the kitchen and took a wrong turn. It'd been a few years since he stepped foot in Taylor's house, and when he did it was never like this. He knew Taylor had a list of chores he was given each day, but you can only dust and vacuum around so much clutter. Cardboard boxes, too many old TVs, engine parts, a piece of plywood on the couch which held lug nuts that'd been spray-painted, with overspray covering the back of the couch.

Everything was dusted, the floor was vacuumed, and as he passed by Taylor's room, he took note of how immaculate it was. Every book in its place, his bed made, clothes put away. Kevin teared up at the thought of his best friend living here with a monster like Jacob Singletree, looming over Taylor, beating him, forcing him to live in this rat cage. Touching him.

Kevin kicked at the wall, and the plaster inside crumbled, cascading down the lath like beans in a rain stick. He kicked again and the wall gave. One more kick and his foot went through. He could do this all day, destroy Jacob's home, but he needed to hurry. Taylor needed him.

He ran to Jacob's room and went straight for the closet, wasting no time searching the floor or back of the closet but went for the shelf up high, which held baseball caps, a pair of old boots, a stack of magazines, porno movies, and a gray lockbox. That had to be it.

He grabbed the thing and shook it. It was full of something, and he imagined if that something was letters, then this is what it would sound like.

On the side of the bed was a nightstand. He searched it for keys and found nothing but lubricant, used tissue, beer caps, and batteries. He lifted the mattress. Nothing. He ran to the front and back doors, searching for a key holder. There was one at the front but the single key on it was too big for the lockbox.

After doing one last look through the man's bedroom and searching his dresser, Kevin decided as long as he had the letters, locked or not, that's all that mattered.

As he stopped at the window and stuck his foot through, he saw a fist-sized hole in the wall, bits of drywall lay on the floor underneath it. Next to the mess was a crumpled piece of paper covered in duct tape with four words written on it that brought a prideful smile to his face.

Dear Jacob,

Fuck you!

CHAPTER 29

BY THE TIME Kevin arrived back at the fort, Taylor had gotten worse. His mouth had sealed shut, with barely any resemblance of ever having one, and two of the fingers on his right hand had begun to meld together.

Kevin came through the door and looked at Jackie first, scanning him for some semblance of a smile, but his face was a beaten thing that'd seen too much. Eyes swollen, nose red, and eyebrows in a permanent upward arch of worry.

He sat down in front of Taylor with the lockbox in hand. "Are they in here, Tay?"

With Taylor's eye narrowed to a slit, he nodded.

"What are we going to do with them?" Jackie asked.

"Not sure yet, but we got 'em."

Small talk with Taylor was pointless, because Taylor wasn't there. He was tucked inside himself, fading away. Even the piss-filled underwear had finally seeped into flesh, leaving nothing but a slight discoloration from the rest of the pale wax. There was no asking if he wanted a drink or a homemade cookie. No sense in offering a funny story or dirty joke. Nothing could distract him from the disintegration.

"I'll only ask you once, Tay. Do you want us to get help?" Kevin knew it was like asking a man on fire if he'd like a thimble full of water. Whatever turning point there could have been had long since passed.

Taylor directed his eye to the notebook.

"I already asked him," Jackie said, then scooted the notebook toward Kevin, where he saw everything Taylor had written.

Taylor reached for the notebook, and tried snapping his fingers, but it made no sound.

Jackie handed him the pen. "You wanna write?"

Taylor attempted to nod, but it was more of a wiggle that caused his whole body to move.

Taylor began to scribble out words on the paper, taking his time with each letter as his pincer-like hand shook.

Thank you for being my friends

Both boys choked up as their eyes bulged with tears, nostrils flared, and chins dimpled.

And for never making fun of me

It was Kevin's turn to hold his friend, breaking into sobs that resembled screams. Taylor threw his arm around him, patted his shoulder, then went back to writing in the notebook.

When Kevin released his hold and leaned back, he read the note and his mouth flew open, the skin between his eyes folding into a symbol of confusion and fear.

Make it so I can't breathe

Please!

"Oh God, Tay!" Jackie cried.

Kevin fixated on the words, trying to give them a different meaning than what they clearly meant. He entertained which was worse, ending the suffering, or the selfish act of doing nothing. The scenario was incomprehensible, murdering your best friend at their request. An act of love so disguised as evil that no matter what they did, guilt would haunt them forever.

The two boys looked intently at their friend and the very small part of him that still existed.

Taylor blinked his drying eye and it stuck there, melding before them. Kevin quickly pried the lids apart with his thumbs, and Taylor jerked with resistance, whether due to pain or wanting the flesh to consume him, Kevin couldn't tell. His skin had become truly clay-like, soft and moldable.

The lid dripped with membranous string, and Kevin did his best to wipe it away. It was useless, like brushing away the fringe from a pair of denim cut-offs. He gave Taylor another hug, holding the back of his head and squeezing tight, thinking of every adventure they'd ever had together. The other forts before The Pantheon II, like the one by the creek where they drank daily until they learned about parasites in school and Jackie refused to go anywhere near there again. The miles of bike trails, packed by hours of riding. Swimming at the gravel pits, using a vine from the tree as a swing until it broke. The campfires. The hikes. The time the town had a blackout, and they went door-to-door on a wild scavenger hunt searching for a list of the most absurd things, only to be chased off by dogs, too scared to finish. And the stories. So many stories, some of which caused nightmares, and some which caused contentment. No one wrote like Taylor, and Kevin had said on more than one occasion that Taylor would be a famous writer one day. But this story he would never be able to tell, the most heart-wrenching of them all.

Before letting go, Kevin whispered in Taylor's ear: "You're the best friend I'll ever have."

Kevin wiped his eyes and sat on the ground, face hidden by his hands. Jackie did the same, mumbling quiet prayers or declarations of self-blame, it wasn't clear.

The scuffling sound of stirring cloth and shifting dirt brought their heads back up.

Taylor had managed to turn himself over, burying his face within the blankets, his one arm tucked under the mass of pasty flesh.

"Tay!" Jackie leaned forward, but Kevin held him back. "Tay, don't!"

Taylor's head swayed slowly back and forth, as though trying to burrow or destroy his clay face altogether. The wet, asthmatic sound of Taylor's body searching for breath while he refused it entry filled the fort. This memory would be triggered for years to come whenever the boys slurped the last bit of drink with a straw or heard the emphysemic cough from the elderly.

What should have been Taylor's legs kicked out, while the mass wriggled and spasmed.

Jackie fell back into Kevin's arms and looked away, burying his own face, while Kevin watched Taylor writhe like a maggot, fighting the selfish urge to grab him and mold his face into something that could speak, poke holes into his melting nose so he could breathe, anything to let him live another miserable hour.

After what felt like days, the wheezing and whistling stopped, as did the worm-like wriggling.

"Come on, Jackie." Kevin stood, pulling his friend with him. They headed out the door and down a row of corn, where they stopped and exchanged no words for a full two minutes. Kevin grabbed a cornstalk, uprooted it with a grunt, and threw it as far as he could, growling at the sky.

Jackie did the same.

Stalks and dirt and husks flew for the next several minutes, and by the time they were done—hands cut and arms sore—thirty stalks were pulled and launched across the rows, the sky filled with the screams of two boys crushed by the weight of grief.

Jackie collapsed on the ground, full of sweat and the itchy dander of husks and leaves. He wiped the matting curls from his forehead and said, "What do we do?"

Kevin said nothing.

"Does it make us bad friends?"

"Fuck no."

Jackie grabbed a nearby husk and picked at the tassel.

Kevin sat down next to him and poked at bits of corn scattered in the dirt. "Remember that time we went fishing and Taylor caught that carp with just a piece of corn, and we didn't think he could do it?"

"Yeah. That mother was huge."

"And then he threw it back, said it was too big to die and deserved to keep going if it made it that long."

"I woulda kept it," Jackie said.

"Yeah, me too."

Jackie's eyes widened. "What about when he wrote three different stories for Mrs. Vonavich's class, and we each picked one and turned them in and we all got A's."

"She had to have known."

"Yeah, probably."

There was silence for a while as they each reflected and poured over countless memories.

"You think we shoulda broke the oath?" Jackie asked.

"I don't know that it woulda made a difference, other than him being alone in the hospital, hooked up to machines, and the doctors woulda kept him alive just cuz they ain't ever seen anything like it, and he would have suffered forever like that. All alone."

"But…he's alone right now." The words hung like a dark cloud that might never go away.

CHAPTER 30

THE DOOR CREAKED *open, and the beast entered. Instead of cowering on the bed, the boy ran to the far corner. He couldn't afford to bring attention to the window. Not when he was this close to freedom.*

He threw himself on the ground, bringing his knees to his chest.

"Get up, pussy," the beast growled.

Reluctantly, the boy stood, and the beast swung, hitting the boy square in the eye. His head grew dizzy, and he fell to the floor.

"Quit it with your foolish noises," the beast said. "I'm going to bed now."

The boy felt his eye, which had swelled shut, and the beast stormed out, then slammed the door. The chain rattled, and the key clicked inside the lock.

The boy crawled to the bed. He decided to wait until he thought the beast was asleep before cawing again. He knew once the thing's eyes grew heavy and it began to dream it would stay asleep for the night, for the boy had smelled the heavy taint of ale on its breath.

The wait was nearly unbearable, but he needed to be patient. If this wasn't done right, he would never leave. He would lose all hope, and the freedom he dreamt about would never come.

Finally, as the sun peaked above him, he called for the birds once more.

One bird came and began pecking at the gruel-covered bars, switching from one to another. Its beak alone was an intimidating thing that no doubt could lop a hand off at the wrist should you dare get too close.

Then another bird came and did the same, peck peck pecking away with its massive beak. Before long, the bars set within the heavy brick walls began to weaken and rattle loosely in their holes. Finally, one of the bars fell quietly onto the bed, then another, and another still.

"Thank you," the boy found himself saying. He stood on the bed, and the birds flew away, leaving the window with one bar left, which the boy pulled at with his horribly weak hand. But when the bar finally gave, it sailed across the room and landed on the hard floor, clanging about as loud as thunder.

This would surely wake the beast.

The boy quickly reached for the window's ledge and began to pull himself up, his muscles shaking. He made little progress before he heard the pounding footsteps beyond the door.

He heaved himself up and kicked at the air, while the chain rattled behind him.

The door swung open, and the beast roared with anger, charging the boy's dangling legs. But as it drew close, the sun's rays shot through and sizzled the beast's flesh, throwing it to the floor.

The boy found leverage, kicked out again, and flew through the window, landing on the soft grass.

Behind him, the beast thrashed with rage. The dungeon cell filled with smoke and the scent of burning flesh.

The boy wiggled his toes in the bright green grass, then sprang forward toward the vast field up ahead.

The birds seemed to sing a new song as he ran, like a warm welcome home. The flowers in the field opened as though greeting him, and as he ran through them, they seemed to dance in the breeze as though celebrating the fact he was finally free.

CHAPTER 31

KEVIN AND JACKIE walked down the row of corn and toward the fort, taking their time. It felt like there were gallows up ahead and punishment was afoot. Punishment for telling lies and staying the night in the middle of a cornfield. And for keeping an oath sacred.

Kevin put his hand on the door, looked at Jackie. Nothing needed to be said. This was telepathic. They were in this together—the grief, and whatever comes after.

He pulled the door open.

They walked in and dropped to their knees at Taylor's side. The glimmering sheen of his skin had gone and now held a grayish-blue hue. Each of the boys rested a hand on him, searching for life there. Nothing. In a matter of just a few days, they'd gone from celebrating the most amazing fort that's ever been built, to this—a scar so wide and so deep it would never heal.

Jackie cried harder than Kevin. Kevin's grief had turned to anger. This was much more than the death of their companion. Taylor had been robbed of joy and love and contentment by an abusive father who never deserved him.

"We need to stay here again tonight," Kevin said. "Tell your mom you're staying at my place. We'll need another shovel, your wagon, and those letters."

"What for?" Jackie asked, wiping yet more tears away.

"We need to make things right."

CHAPTER 32

THEY LEFT TAYLOR there inside the fort and didn't say a word to anyone about what had happened. After each speaking to their parents about staying an extra night with the other, they headed out.

Just before dark, Jackie hooked an old, rusted Radio Flyer wagon to the seat post of his bike with rope, then tossed a shovel inside and left for Wagner's field.

Kevin was already in the fort, reading aloud from *The Thief of Always*, where Jackie had left a bookmark between the pages.

They'd covered Taylor's body before leaving that afternoon and planned to never look again. Kevin wanted the memory erased of Taylor's outlandish disfigurement, and seeing the spots where blood chose to pool and turn black would only challenge the effort more.

The sound of hard rubber wheels and rusted axles sounded in the distance. Kevin finished the paragraph he was reading, closed the book, and greeted Jackie outside.

Jackie hopped off his bike and tugged at his shirt. "What if we get caught on the way?"

Kevin thought a moment. "We tell the truth, then lie a little and say we were on our way to the police."

"I'm not even scared, Kev."

"Me either."

And they weren't. Nothing else mattered that night other than redemption.

"My mom made us brownies, but I didn't bring 'em."

"Not hungry anyway."

"Me neither."

It was awkward small talk between two strangers who didn't know where to start. While they both shared the same tremendous grief, there was a loneliness deep down in each of them—an area that battled thoughts with its own unique set of weapons.

Jackie looked at the sky, squinted. "You think there's more meteors? Like just a whole shower of them and they'll land all over the world and—"

"No."

"Just the one? Seems kinda unfair. Almost like it was meant for one of us, like God was playin' a joke."

"What if it was God helping? Like he was stopping the suffering to come?"

"Then it shoulda hit his dad, straight in the balls."

Kevin couldn't argue with that. "Maybe it just happened cuz that's how life is sometimes. I dunno, Jackie."

As the boys stared at the sky in silence, the long pine shadows disappeared while the sun said goodnight, and the crickets began their serenade.

It was time to go.

CHAPTER 33

THE BOYS STOOD beside their bikes at the edge of the cornfield next to a road that led to residential neighborhoods—nearly a mile from the Singletree house.

"If anyone says anything or yells at us, unless it's a cop, don't stop. Just keep riding like you didn't even hear 'em," Kevin said, holding tight to the lockbox full of confessional letters.

Jackie nodded, then sat on his bike, the wagon behind him.

"And no sharp turns. Go wide."

"Got it."

They pulled onto the street, pedaling slowly. The wagon seemed impossibly loud on the paved road, as though it was alerting the houses up ahead of the blanket-wrapped body inside. The two shovels jutting out from under the bundle didn't help the curiously morbid visual. None of it looked good.

As they came upon the first house, their eyes darted about, searching every shadow. A dog barked from within a fenced yard, nearly scaring Jackie off his bike. He swerved, and the wagon threatened to tip. A shovel slipped out and clanged on the street.

They both stopped, and Kevin grabbed the shovel, carefully tucked it back in.

A porch light went on, exposing them. Jackie scuffed his feet on the road and threw his weight on the pedal. The wagon screamed announcements to look over here, sketchy shit is going on.

Kevin rode behind him, keeping his eyes on the wagon and the contents within, watching the corpse of his friend bounce on the rusted Radio Flyer like some giant jumping bean. He hated the way they had unwittingly wrapped him up like a larva, making the dehumanization even worse.

The first turn came, and Jackie took it slow and wide, riding past a man bent over his car in a brightly-lit garage. It made Kevin think of his own father and the sacred memory-building safe haven of light that poured from his garage. The type of sentimental imagery Taylor never got to experience. Instead, any sign Taylor's dad was nearby was lava in his belly and a spine full of spiders, wondering if he'd soon get a beating. Or worse.

Another dog yelped, and Jackie kept his calm, white-knuckling the handlebars to ensure the wheel was kept straight, dodging the occasional pothole.

With the exception of one turn, the ride was a straight shot, and after ten minutes of careful paranoia, the sign up ahead signaled Peck Street was there, a dead-end dirt road.

Jackie took a wide turn, slowed, then planted his feet. Kevin coasted up next to him.

"Maybe we should dump the bikes and pull it through the grass from here," Jackie said. "I think the road's too bumpy."

There were still seven houses between them and the Singletree house, with gravel and paved driveways splitting the lawns.

"Let's keep riding 'til we hit the neighbor's, then stash the bikes in the trees. Just go slow."

While one side of Peck Street contained lower-to-mid class ranch-style homes, the other was filled with dense trees—a forest the boys once spoke of building bike trails through, but Taylor wasn't keen to the idea of being that close to home, something Kevin didn't understand at the time. But after a while, he realized that just like Taylor used books to escape, getting away from anything that resembled life at home was another form of escapism, and those trees were nothing but the background of a painting he never wanted to look at.

They rode down the street without incident. Surprisingly, the dirt road muted some of the rusted cacophony, while the trees absorbed some more, as though working as a team, privy to the boys' plan.

Near the edge of the property next to Taylor's, the boys jumped off their bikes. Jackie untied the rope, and they dumped their bikes across the street among the shadows, just inside the woods.

"There's a break in those hedges." Kevin pointed toward the side of the neighbor's yard. "We'll pull the wagon through there."

Jackie pulled the wagon on his own, and while the grass was much quieter than the road, the wheels squealed under the weight of the cargo, and the slower they went, the louder they were. For the remainder of the short way there, he picked up the pace, watching for the illumination of sudden porch lights or moving shadows, then parked the wagon alongside the hedges near the opening, while Kevin went through and looked in the driveway, searching for Jacob's Impala, then came back.

"Okay, he's not home. But the wagon's too loud. Leave it here."

"Carry him?" Jackie asked, but Kevin had already begun to grab one end of Taylor, which end he couldn't tell, until he felt the protruding shoulder of Taylor's right arm, the only part of him that went untouched by the transformation.

Jackie grabbed the other end. The shovels clanged in the wagon, and one fell out onto the grass. They both swung their heads toward the neighbor's house and held their breath, waiting to be spotlighted or hear the sound of a screen door opening.

Nothing.

"Okay," Kevin said. "On three."

On the count of three, they lifted their friend's wrapped body. Whether it be the rigor mortis or the natural fusion of Taylor's limbs, the handling of his corpse was easier to handle than Kevin anticipated. Once they found their balance and Jackie signaled he was ready, they carried Taylor through the gap in the hedges, Kevin leading the way, walking backward.

Once through, he nodded toward the backyard. "Behind the garage," he whispered.

Kevin began to dwell on the morbidity of the situation, the surrealism, and the absurdity, then shut it down quick before he dropped the body and ran, leaving his deceased friend in the driveway of a house he just as soon set on fire, with Jacob Singletree in it.

Jackie huffed and blew the sweaty curls from his brow as he took short but quick steps.

Once behind the garage, they gently set Taylor's body down. Jackie bent over, put his hands on his knees, catching his breath, while Kevin ran back to the wagon and grabbed the shovels.

A rowboat sat leaning horizontally against the back of the garage. It hadn't been used in years, and Kevin wondered if this was the vessel that brought Mrs. Singletree to her ultimate death, as it was the middle of Meyer Lake that she drowned. Jacob had claimed she slipped and fell during a fishing trip and despite his best effort, couldn't save her, stating she had never even surfaced and sank like a rock. He'd made the obligatory panicked call to EMS, and two weeks later she was found bloated and beached on the far side of the lake. Despite Jacob's reputation, not one person pointed a suspecting finger his way. Whether that had something to do with his escalating alcoholism disguised as grief and the locals' sympathy for his loss, or because the idea of murder in Springview was just too much to grasp, Kevin wasn't sure. But in hindsight, he felt like a fool never considering Jacob was at fault and felt everyone else should feel the same. And one day soon, they would.

"Help me move the boat," Kevin said.

They moved it down several feet, and Kevin pointed toward the giant spot of black earth where no grass had grown. "We'll dig here, then put the boat back."

Jackie took a moment to look at his surroundings. Even in the middle of the day nobody could have seen them. But them hearing the sound of shoveling dirt late into the night was a curiosity most might deem worthy of investigating.

Fortunately, the dirt was soft, and the grave would be shallow. Jackie huffed and had to rest twice, while Kevin continued, fueled by pure adrenaline. He explained to Jackie that a shallow grave would work best and assured him this would not be Taylor's final resting place. When the hole was nearly five feet long and only two feet deep, they stopped.

Jackie looked down at the bulging blanket. "We should say some words."

"Of course."

Jackie gathered a mouth full of dirt-tainted phlegm and spit it into the bushes, then swallowed. "Tay… I'm sorry for pulling you in that old, shitty wagon like that." Then he began to sob, the next few sentences barely audible. "I'm sorry about everything, Tay. But we're gonna make things right." He wiped his eyes, then took a step back as though signaling to Kevin it was his turn.

Kevin stalled a moment, took a deep breath. "Tay. I never told you this, but… I always wanted to be like you. Smart and everything, reading books and knowing all those cool facts. But I don't think I ever will be, cuz you had something you just can't learn from books. I don't know what it's called, but you had it." Kevin teared up but held back the best he could. "Thank *you* for being our friend… and for never making fun of us."

Jackie whimpered and sniffled behind him.

"Sorry about this, Tay." Then Kevin put his hand on Jackie's shoulder. "Let's do it."

As they began rolling Taylor's body into the hole, the blanket unraveled and Taylor spilled out, landing in the bottom of the hole. Before either boy had a chance to grimace at the way his head cocked up at them, faceless, headlights flashed across the yard, and the rumble of Jacob Singletree's Impala came to a halt on the other side of the garage.

CHAPTER 34

THEY FROZE.

The Impala door opened on a hinge that screamed like a banshee, and Jackie pissed his pants. He gripped his penis and tried cutting off the flow, silently chanting *NO!* over and over again, but it didn't help.

Kevin dropped to his knees and shut his eyes, willing the man to go inside and pass out in bed under the loud whir of his air conditioner. Or fall and break his neck.

The banshee screamed again, and the door slammed.

Footsteps. Louder, then distant.

The spring on the screen door sounded—a chorus of angels.

"Hurry," Kevin whispered. He grabbed the lockbox, set it next to Taylor, and began pushing the mounds of dirt into the hole with his hands, trying not to look at his dead friend.

Jackie started crying and covered his mouth, then stumbled to the bushes and vomited.

Kevin continued to fill the hole as fast as he could. Before long, all but the top of Taylor's head was covered. Jackie wiped his mouth, his eyes, and came back to help. A loud commotion came from within the house—the banging of pots and pans, doors, or beer bottles, it wasn't clear. But Jacob did not sound happy.

Once the hole was filled, the boys stomped on the dirt, the ground sinking under them. Jackie mewled and whispered pleas of forgiveness, while Kevin grabbed a shovel and filled the sunken spots until it was flat, then the two pounded it with their feet once more before flattening the earth with the shovels and wiping their footprints away.

They moved the boat back over the grave, grabbed the shovels, then crept around the side of the garage and peeked at the house. Lights were on inside, but there was no sign of Jacob.

"Go," Kevin said, and they quietly followed the shadows along the garage and down the driveway, footsteps like mice.

"Hey!" Jacob Singletree called out from one of the windows, his voice damning and thunderous. "Who the fuck are you?"

The boys wasted no time in bolting, as though shot from a cannon or lit on fire, and if Jackie still had piss left in him, he didn't anymore.

"The fuck you doin' out there?"

As they cleared the hedge and ran past the wagon, Jackie yelled, "Fuck yooouu!"

The back porch light lit the yard, and something in the house crashed behind them. A door slammed, and the screen door sang. By this time, they were nearly to the street.

"Forget the bikes," Kevin said. "Just hit the woods."

They ran across the street, tossed the shovels among the weeds, and headed into the woods, where tiny branches split skin and left welts that wouldn't be noticed for hours.

Jacob's booming voice grew distant, and the boys finally stopped running. They ducked behind a tree and watched the street from afar. The man stood there, looking down the street for any sign of the short intruders, then gave up and walked back toward his house.

"Don't move," Kevin said. "He could be watching from behind the hedge."

"He's gonna go back there and see that we were diggin', and we'll go to jail. Oh man… we failed Taylor." Jackie was nearly hyperventilating, cradling his stomach.

"No, we didn't. We're fine."

"We need to call the police right now then."

"We can't. If they dig him up now, they'll never accuse his dad. Not the way his body… you know what I'm saying."

"So… we have to wait until he dec—… I can't say it." Jackie looked at the ground.

"You don't know the word?"

"I know the word. I just can't say it. I won't."

"Yeah. We have to wait."

"How long?"

"I don't know. Until there's mostly just bones."

Jackie shook his head, like he wanted nothing to do with the conversation.

"Come on." Kevin headed toward the road and their bikes, crouching. "Don't mess around, just get on your bike, haul ass, and meet at McKinley. If he chases us, split up. Cut through yards if you have to."

Jackie swallowed hard. "Got it."

All eyes were on the hedges and the black gap between them. The wagon sat there like a witness they'd have to leave behind. With luck, the neighbors would get rid of it, thinking it was nothing but another piece of junk from the Singletree home, and not a makeshift hearse.

The bike rims glimmered up ahead, and the boys picked up their pace. Still no sign of Taylor's father. When they saw the glow of the back-porch light turn off, they ran, hopped on their bikes, and pedaled as fast as they could away from a house they'd never visit or call again.

They rode down two other streets before stopping at McKinley Park. They parked their bikes alongside trees and sat on swings. Between the moon and a nearby streetlight, the park was lit adequately, peacefully.

"We did it," Jackie said, sitting in his own piss.

"Yeah."

"Taylor would have done the same for us, huh?"

"Yeah, he would."

They sat quietly, each of them reflecting. Kevin tried not to think about the way Taylor had looked in that hole, his one arm reaching out for freedom from his own body. He twisted the image into something beautiful—a chrysalis. The early stages of freedom soon to come, just before the butterfly emerges, stretches its wings, and takes flight. That was Taylor now. Free and flying.

EPILOGUE

KEVIN AND JACKIE stood in the cemetery, Taylor's headstone at their feet. They'd visited often that month, taking turns reading out loud from *The Thief of Always*. This time, they read the final page and set the book on the stone.

Jackie dug a small hole in the ground with a spoon, just deep enough to bury three pieces of paper, covered front and back with the last story Taylor ever wrote. A story that seemed to reveal its true meaning the more they read it.

"Your best one yet." Jackie said.

"Definitely," Kevin agreed.

"Kevin's been going out with Kristy Spencer for a whole six months now. Can you believe it? I'll bet they get married." Jackie eyes were on the small headstone.

Kevin hit Jackie with a playful punch. "But I haven't told her about The Pantheon Two, Tay. Oath keepers, right?"

"Oath keepers." Jackie repeated.

"Well..." Kevin touched the flat stone, the embossed letters that said *Beloved Friend*, then shed a tear like he always did when saying goodbye, knowing the goodbyes would never end.

Jackie's eyes glistened. He blinked the tears away and patted Kevin on the back, then pulled him toward the grave next to Taylor's. Jacob Singletree's grave. A coward, unwilling to pay for his sins, preferring a bullet to the temple over spendinghad even a single night in prison, reflecting on the monster he was. No alcohol to hide behind. No family to take the blows.

Kevin reached in his backpack and pulled out the 2-liter of piss-vinegar—The Pantheon II gargoyle. The oath-keeping guardian.

He twisted the cap, and a quiet hiss escaped the bottle. The air filled with repugnance, and the boys caught a whiff of the promise-breaker's potion, something they knew none of them would ever have to drink.

Kevin tipped the bottle over Jacob's grave and the contents poured out, darkening the dirt over the man's final resting place. The sun seemed to burn a little brighter then, and somewhere in the distance, the sound of a crow's caw carried through the spring breeze, bringing a smile to each boy's face.

Made in the USA
Middletown, DE
22 January 2025

69162895R00085